The Fear of Knowing

Tisha Starr

Editor: Alanna Boutin

ISBN: 0988979500
ISBN-13: 978-0-9889795-0-5

DEDICATION

This book is dedicated to all the women, men and children battling
with or who have died from HIV/AIDS.

CONTENTS

ACKNOWLEDGMENTS

Without my father in Heaven this project would not have seen the light of day. I am blessed. To my children, I drove you all nuts through the writing process. But you encouraged and gave me the strength to see it through to the end. I thank you so much for loving and believing in me. To my family, blood, extended and chosen, I love you guys so much. You all understand my need to be creative as well as my weirdness but accept me for who I am. And for that, I thank you. And I'd like to extend a special thanks to my entire fundraising committee, you guys were awesome and I couldn't have done it without you. My M.C. tore down the house, the cookie sellers raise that dough and my web designer, you rock! Last but not least, to my special friend who, even in the midst of trouble, made sure I had an awesome book cover and money to finance my project, I thank you!

PROLOGUE

As we ran up the stairs to undress, my heartbeat was visible through the thin silk cami drizzled across my chest. I was anxious. It was my very first time. I should have been happy, but I wasn't—just anxious. I wanted it. I wanted him badly. Ty and I worked long and hard in the backseat of my truck to build an exotic feeling I tried hard not to lose; but guilt squirmed its way into my thoughts at the same rate the juices flowed below my waist. Didn't I deserve to enjoy womanhood, I questioned myself.

It isn't my fault Dad screwed me over, I thought in an attempt to welcome my natural sexual desires. But the more I thought about it, the worse I felt. Moisture between my legs dampened the pink boy shorts I wore. It felt like a mass of butterflies were let loose below, trying frantically to escape.

As we reached the top of the stairs, I felt Ty's warm, strong hands clasp my waist, gently swirling me about until our faces connected. "Are you sure you want to do this, Tasha?" he whispered, as his hand swept softly across my lower back. Instantly, a flow of fluid nestled in my panties.

"D-a-m-n-," I burst out in a soft breath.

"Damn what?" Ty asked.

I answered his question with a passionate kiss. It felt good to suck his lips and twirl my tongue inside his warm mouth. As our lips broke apart I asked worriedly, "Did you bring the condoms?"

"Yes, babe. Find something else to worry your pretty little head about. I will not turn you—no, us—into teenage parents, I promise," he assured me.

Waving my pointer finger seductively, I signaled Ty to follow me into my cozy bedroom while I went to freshen up.

My room was spotless, lights already dimmed. I kept them that way on a regular basis. A circular king-size bed dressed in yellow satin sheets decorated the floor, while the aroma of Hawaiian scents bounced from wall to wall. I popped a smooth groove CD into the six-disk changer and it played on repeat softly in the background. Ty was probably in the room feeling like he won millions, I thought to myself as I scurried down the hall in pure excitement.

Closing the bathroom door with my mind focused on losing my virginity, I studied my reflection in the full-body mirror. It was different than normal. The small timid girl with tiny boobs became the faint background to a developing photo. Right before my eyes, my childhood's blotchy brown skin, flat forehead, and chubby cheeks was blotted out by my wide hips, and even-toned skin, confirming my passage into womanhood.

I placed one hand on each hip and turned slightly to the left to catch a glimpse of my butt as I examined one body part per every couple seconds after another. A transformation was happening. I was about to become a woman.

At once my stare halted at the eyes peering back at me through the glass and dad's countless lectures zapped into my mind like a transmitter. Each word trampled my brain with great force, overtaking my sexual needs and interrupting the flow.

"Tasha, you aren't like other little girls. You are

3

special. The birds and the bees story had to be rewritten for a pretty girl like you. Please don't tell our secret. It will turn your best friend into your worst enemy, that's just how the world goes. This is a burden that you have to carry alone; don't put someone you love in your position. You could lose everything. Always remember, I love you dearly."

Bullshit. I snapped out of my daze and not only were my panties wet, so was my face. "If you loved me so fucking much, then why can't I live a normal damn life?" I questioned the air.

Ty thinks I don't want to become another teenage statistic, but the truth is I'm a coward, a goddamn coward. I can't gather enough courage to tell my new best friend my dad was a weak motherfucker. According to Daddy, "He was sorry." And that he was.

Just as a full-blown breakdown was about to happen, I pictured Ty's dark brown skin. He wasn't the tallest, but you could imagine his body on any man in *Maxim*. The thought of Ty's light brown eyes, perfect teeth, and stubby ears made me moist all over again. A knock on the door startled me as I scrambled to clean my face.

"Don't come in. I'm not dressed," I lied.

"That's just how I want you to be," Ty said, gliding his body into the room like a king. "What's wrong, babe? Getting cold feet? Are you in here crying," he asked as he wiped the glistening streaks from my face with the back of his hand, holding my cheeks in his palms.

"Nothing, I'm cool. I just don't want to lose my virginity today, Ty. My punk ass chickened out," I said, attempting to joke my way through the pain. We laughed and hugged in the middle of the bathroom floor.

"Well, then, it's settled. You get to keep it for one more day, but tomorrow that ass is mine." Ty slapped my booty while staring at it like it was a prized possession.

We left the bathroom amused, hands tangled together. I suggested we turn on the TV instead, but when we heard loud moans and spanking sounds come from the speakers, my face was immediately covered with embarrassment.

It was a pretty young woman getting banged from the back on the large screen. Just that quick I had forgotten I watched porn before leaving for school that morning. Until that date, porn and masturbation were the closest thing to sex I'd ever encountered. Ty's eyes landed on my blushing face, and we fell backward on the bed bubbling with laughter.

"Oh, so *that's* what turns you on," he said quickly. "Well, we can watch it since this is what you like." He obviously hadn't surrendered that easy. Truthfully, I couldn't take another minute of the video. My insides felt like a motor was left running, and my nipples stood up. Ty studied my body and one long stare at my cami and he knew I was physically ready to lose my gift, but mentally unprepared. Little did he know my vagina was hardly a gift. It was a poison apple. Well, at least that's what I thought it was.

In a sexy, deep voice, he said, "Just lay back and let me talk to you, Tasha. My hands speak another language."

"I don't wanna hear your hands speak sex talk," I giggled.

"*Shh,*" he said. My body froze in intimidation as he held one hand over my mouth and used the other to graze across my breast. I couldn't say another word. He eased his large, warm, pouted lips to one nipple, sucking tenderly, causing my body to maneuver in figure eight motions. Releasing his hand from my moaning lips, one finger at a time, he gently explored my nervous but well-developed body. Ty pursued his exploration with hard gripping and slow massaging motions; rubbing in and out of my physical and mental state. I was losing it. I loved him, and he knew it. Just as I was about to scream out in ecstasy, "I Love You, Tyrone Johnson!" he pulled me close to him, my hard breasts pressed against his sculpture, looked through my pupils and into my soul, and said, "I love you, Tasha Davis."

It was over—I was going through with *it*.

I didn't have to ask again about the condom. Like the gentleman he always portrayed himself to be, when I looked down, his manhood was half draped in lubricated latex as he rolled the remainder down his penis. I suggested we use two. "You know, better safe than sorry," I said nervously.

Ty had a confused look on his face but honored my request. "Whatever it takes to make your first time memorable, I will do, baby girl. Even if it means wearing two suffocating condoms," he said.

I was madly in love. As he entered my being, I closed my eyes and everything I ever could imagine came true: that my father was indeed alive, my mother was truly my best friend, and I was HIV-negative.

1 TASHA DAVIS – M54215

Today, I felt really cold in the tiny concrete room that had been my home the past four-hundred and twelve days. The paper-thin itchy jail blanket wrapped around me didn't break the chill and allowed the stinging coldness to spread like a plague over my body.

I had memorized the placement of every scratch, hole, tag, pipe, and bar within my cell. If a guard presented a pop quiz on the locations of any object within that space, I would ace it.

Staring at the ceiling, I daydreamed about my release date that was rapidly approaching. "What will I do," I questioned "and how shall I do it?" Answers were few and far in between.

But what I did know was long, long ago I gave up all

efforts to understand why I was locked away in the first place; I promised myself to never spend another minute thinking about that uselessness. It was plain to see that a deeper understanding couldn't change the opinions of others towards me or my past. To those that judged me, the hard part was almost over. And according to my accuser and the other twelve men and women that decided my fate, after my fourteen month jail sentence ends, I should be "reformed."

"Ha, another batch of bull I've been dealt in my lifetime," I mumbled underneath my breath. "How in the hell can you reform my illness? I'm pretty sure every HIV-positive person across the globe is awaiting that answer. There would be lines forming outside of penitentiaries all over the place if jail time was the magic cure," I spoke aloud to the four walls that never, ever responded to me.

Hmm, the world, this crazy world, never understood I've been in jail within my own body all of my life. No one knew that being confined to a tiny concrete room could never compare to the reinforced steel beam I constructed inside my heart. How can you lock me away from myself, I wondered.

"Tasha, you have a visitor," the sheriff said from the

gate, interrupting the one-woman pity party which was just beginning in my cell. I really didn't want to see anyone. That time was needed to prepare for the next day.

Tomorrow would be the first chance I got to speak out publicly and willingly about my life. Tomorrow was the day of my atonement. Although my prison time did nothing to help the issues I had like my persecutors believed it would, the sole lesson I did reap was to give up on the *fear of people knowing.*

"Tasha, it's Ty," Patrice said.

Patrice was one of the nicer guards who always looked out for me. The other ones treated me like a number, not a person. Every day she tried to make sure I was as comfortable as I could be under the circumstances. "You remind me so much of my daughter," she would often say.

My heart leaped, flipped, and placed itself back in its rightful spot in my chest from the sound of Ty's name. He still held that power, and I refused to give it up.

Looking into the plastic mirror super glued to the wall that made me appear fatter than I actually was, I brushed my hair and cleared my eyes of its crusty edges. Patrice signaled for me to follow her through the cold corridors and into the holding area where I was stripped from head to toe, told to bend over, cough two times, and redress—you know, common procedure. After being cleared of not concealing any weapons or contraband, I was escorted to my table where Ty, looking luscious as usual, was already seated.

The visiting room was the size of a small banquet hall minus beautification. Long, elementary-style lunchroom tables covered every inch of the open floor plan. It had the appearance of a 1970s classroom; it was that old and that ugly. I guess it was comfortable enough for state workers, or so they were led to believe.

Chitter-chatter consumed the area and swallowed up any aspect of individuality. Every conversation became the business of people at neighboring tables because there is no such thing as privacy in prison. You would find out who slept with whom, what beauty shop got the most business, and who was murdered, raped, or arrested in the latest drug sting. But the most heartbreaking image was of children asking, "mommy, mommy, when are you coming home?" Most jailhouse women answered identically, "Soon honey, real soon," which was hardly ever the truth. I tried to block out as much as I could and focus on Ty.

"Hey, Tasha," Ty greeted me cheerfully. With my head

hung low I responded, "Hey, Ty." Although I loved him dearly, I found it difficult to understand why he would want to be in my presence.

"I got your letter, so the big day is tomorrow. Are you ready?"

"No, actually, I'm not. This will be the first time since Jamia that I opened up, and I'm terrified." Like always, Ty assured, reassured, and guaranteed me that it was time for this to happen and that I could do it. He was one amazing young man.

"So, are you sure you have no fear of people knowing your side of the story," I asked unwillingly. "Ty you know I won't disclose any of your information without your permission."

"Must we go through this again, Tasha," Ty said confidently. "I don't care what people think about me anymore. What I care about is helping others, and if exposing our story can do that—then so be it." I could tell he got a bit agitated by the question because so far, that's all our letters were ever about. I thanked him and dropped the subject.

"I brought you something," Ty said, as he leaned his body backward in the chair, giving himself enough room to fit his hand in his jean pocket. "Don't open this until you get back to your cell. It's a token of good luck."

I took the paper from his cold hands and placed it in the small square pocket of my orange jail suit. Looking deeply in his eyes I whispered, "I won't open it."

We stared at each other for a few seconds searching for a conversation. We decided a few weeks earlier not to talk anymore about why I failed to tell him my status before we had sex. He explained that in order for him to learn not to hate me, the first step was to stop talking about the problem and work toward a solution. I could tell that he still hated *it*, the act, but was trying seriously to find forgiveness in his heart for *me*, the person. Tyrone was wise beyond his years.

Quickly, and in a concerned manner, he asked, "Has your mother been down to see you?"

"Yes, babe..." I caught myself, "I mean, yeah Ty." My mother has really tried to support me through this, but you know her. She peered back and forth between her watch and the clock during the entire visit."

"Well, just give her some time. You know she never knew anything besides her work. She'll come around." He filled me in about our friends back home that I lost contact with, and how our neighborhood was changing with bigger houses, less black folk.

In my mind, I could care less about lower income people being pushed out for richer ones, but since it was important to him, it was important to me. I had deeper issues than being concerned about the zoning of new communities. I told myself I wouldn't ask questions that would shift the tone of our visits from positive to negative, but there was one thing that disturbed me since the day I was arrested. I had to ask.

"Ty," I said quietly and with a brief pause, not sure if I wanted to hear the answer, "does your mother still hate me?"

"Tasha, I thought we weren't—"

"Five more minutes," the sheriff shouted just as the conversation was about to take flight. Ty finished his statement after the announcement everyone hated to hear. "I thought we weren't going to worry about anyone else right now other than ourselves and our health."

"You're right, this isn't about other people. I guess I better take these last five minutes to say how much I appreciate you coming all this way to see me."

"You're welcome. As hard as it is for me to work through my own personal emotions right now, I don't want to abandon you like the rest of the world, and to me, that's all that should matter."

I smiled as we both stood up at the same time and planted my rough, untreated lips on the side of his face. Then I wrapped my arms snuggly behind his body telling him "Good-bye and thanks again for coming."

"You're welcome," he replied without similar acts of affection. The visit was over.

On the way back to the cell I thought of ways to tire out my mind and body as preparation for a good night's sleep. I don't remember anything else but waking up to the nurse with my cocktail of daily meds.

The weather was beautiful and breakfast on that day wasn't so bad. I ate everything, which was unusual for me. My goal was to have a full stomach before taking the pills that made me nauseous the first hour or two after ingestion. If I took the pills right after breakfast and before morning shower, my stomach didn't react as viciously. Maybe the water was a type of soothing relief, but who knows. I made sure my orange suit was pressed extra crispy for the special occasion and took advantage of the jailhouse beautician who rocked my hair the day before.

While putting the finishing touches on my bangs, the

beautician, in her thugged-out voice, said, "Let these fools know you ain't no damn criminal, these punk-ass motherfuckers. I hate the system. I'm glad you get to tell your story."

We laughed. "No doubt," I told her.

The transport bus came at 10:00 A.M. to take me to the county building where I was asked to deliver a speech at a victim impact panel. It was on the bus that I remembered the letter Ty gave me in the visiting room. Almost ripping the cheap pocket off my jumpsuit, I pulled the letter out anxiously to read what he had written.

Dear Tasha,

I haven't taken the opportunity to tell you how much pain I have suffered since that night. I've battled demon after demon, including suicidal ones, trying to understand what all this means for my future. Yet every time I thought about what we meant to each other before this all occurred, I somehow found a reason to move forward. People tell me all the time that in order to heal from any rip or tear of the heart you have to learn to forgive and forget. In all honesty, I may be light-years away from ever forgetting, but I have come extremely close to forgiveness. I hope my honesty will give you the courage to speak up tomorrow and give an unbiased testimony of your life. Your story, our story, could possibly help a multitude of young men and women facing similar challenges.

Sincerely,

Tyrone Johnson

My heart was full. I could not control the eruption of emotions from the pit of my heart that spilled onto my face. What Ty didn't know was we battled similar demons—especially the suicidal one. But the simple thought of him forgiving me gave me the strength I needed to move forward. I gazed out of the bus window at greenery I hadn't seen in over a year and thought to myself, *Go get 'em, tiger.*

I walked full of fear to the front of the room as the crowd gazed upon me with unforgiving eyes. Any minute now I would be eaten alive, I worried. To my left, I overheard a teenage girl say, "Mom, she's gorgeous. There's no way she's sick." I guess my five foot six height, glowing dark skin, perfectly shaped figure, and beautiful hairstyle concealed my illness. The girl's mother held her index finger close to her full lips signaling for her to be quiet as the facilitator took center stage.

"The keynote speaker has been transported from a

local penitentiary; she was found guilty in the State of Illinois for Criminal Transmission of HIV. Let us be mindful again that although she's incarcerated, she is here, like all of us, in an attempt to break the stigma surrounding the disease. This young lady was not forced or coerced but came voluntarily to share her story. We will not hesitate asking you to remove yourself from the room if she isn't given the same respect and courtesy as our other panel guest. Please welcome, Tasha Davis."

The applause was so faint, fear and sorrow brewed rapidly in my chest while I timidly approached the podium. As I drew closer to the wooden block, adorned with a gold plate, a woman's sobs attacked me from the back row. It was Ty's mother. My flesh died. Now I stood in a mound of dread and embarrassment; my body seemed to grow a mind of its own as it drifted away from the podium. *I can't do it; I can't stand in front of her and explain how I ruined her son's life,* my thoughts took over.

"No, please," a woman protested from the front of the audience, "don't leave. We wanna' hear from you. You'll be okay. We all make mistakes."

"Mistakes, my ass," I heard another lady groan and grumble. "I would kick her cute behind if she slept with my son."

"Uh-huh," mumbled another in agreement.

"Quiet down, please," the MC scorned. "Go ahead, Tasha."

Just as the negativity clogging up the room tried to rob me of my voice, I remembered Ty's letter. I assembled enough strength to look beyond the hateful gazes, bottled-up the feelings welling up inside and pressed on. Three dull sounds escaped my tight lips to clear a lump that crept up the back of my throat. I stared blankly into the crowd, said a silent prayer, and began my journey through life.

"My name is Tasha Davis, and I'm HIV-positive. I have heard your disapprovals, and trust me, they are plentiful. However, today, I've been allowed ninety-minutes to tell you how I ended up in prison. I will attempt to explain why I believe stigmatizing HIV has to end in order for us to combat this deadly virus. I won't pretend to know all the answers but what I can offer you today is my story. I'm not seeking pity, nor am I begging to be liked or accepted. Yet by the end of my story, I hope you all understand that what happened to me could happen to any one of you, your children, or your loved ones."

The room went silent, no more crumpling of paper,

whispering, or milling about. I felt the weight of the world perched on my neck as I painfully traveled with the audience to the very beginning.

2 HOW IT ALL BEGAN

My mother and I lived in a northwest suburb of
Chicago. Our red, brick home with huge picture windows
and skylights sprawled across half the block. Mother was
creative. My room was perched on the tip of a long,
winding staircase, and she had splattered Elmo decals on
the walls from floor to ceiling.

"Hey, honey," she said, "now you live on Sesame
Street."

I loved Elmo, and that was one thing about me Mother
was sure of; everything else was questionable. Of course,
my mom had to have matching curtains and bedding. That
part didn't matter to me, but to her, beauty was more than
skin-deep.

I spent most of my time in the huge, dense room

overpopulated with toys. My memory is quite deficient prior to my fifth birthday so any information I offer is told from the perspective of my mother. She said that I was sick often from medication and spent more hours in bed than on the floor playing with dolls, trucks, or pets. When I wasn't sick, I passed lots of time away by peering out of the living-room window. Watching the neighborhood children ride their bikes and run about held my interest most of the time, but I never liked them much though. They always found a way to make me feel weird with their long gazes and odd stares.

My mother, Cali, insisted that I not roughhouse with other children anyway. "I just can't afford for you to cut yourself, Tasha," she would say.

Back then, I didn't understand why she dreaded my blood. I thought I was an alien. But it was very different in Chicago at Daddy's house. He let me play until my legs were sore.

One day when I was seven, Mommy came home unexpected, face bright, eyes big, and shaking with eagerness, screaming—"Follow me, Tasha! I have a surprise for you out back."

My heart clanked about and excitement interfered with

my breathing. I closed my eyes and pictured a big, blue aboveground swimming pool with a chrome stepladder. The same one I had circled in different sales papers I left purposely on the kitchen table for weeks. Water was the one thing that didn't make me nauseated. Everything else I was bound to puke from after the motions ceased. I'd always wanted a pool. My heart felt something for Mommy in that moment; I sensed we were finally connecting.

She took me by the hand, and we scurried through the foyer down the hall and toward the back Arcadian doors. "Ta-da," Mother shouted.

I couldn't believe what I was staring at. *My mother is an idiot,* I thought. It was a huge yellow and wooden swing set.

"OK, 1, 2, 3 . . . last one there is a rotten egg," she shouted enthusiastically while sprinting to the swing on the left. I knew the best thing for me was to pretend to be happy and play along with my mother's game. She didn't like unappreciative children, and I vividly remember not being in the mood to be lectured. I jogged to the swing set, smiling halfheartedly.

Mother and I hopped on the swings, pumping and kicking our extended legs aimed at the sky. Just as I lost myself in the pure beauty of outdoors, she jerked me back to reality. "You know what, Tasha? Mommy is the happiest I've been since the day you were born. I wouldn't trade this moment for the world." There was a long pause. "I could just swing out here forever . . ." Her voice sounded distant because at the time I was focused on birds gliding through the air and clouds bumping into one another in the sky to pay any attention to my mother's words, but that didn't stop her from rambling.

"Tasha, honey," she said after another brief pause, "I need you to be a big girl while I work harder to keep this house. Can I trust you to do that?" I don't know how, but my mom was still unaware we were in two different worlds at that moment, she in ecstasy while I struggled to survive in a deep dark pit of disappointment. The words she spoke weren't registering, so she relied on her normal approach and questioned in a stern voice, "DID YOU HEAR ME, Tasha?"

"Yes, Mommy, I will be a big girl while you're at work," I responded instinctively. She had a quick temper, and I didn't want the moment to be ruined because I failed to answer her favorite question. Being a big girl was really her only request of me. And since she worked all the time it was all I knew how to do anyhow.

I soon found out her demand was really different that time and it had a brand new meaning. Purchasing the swing set was Mother's way of telling me her businesses and home were more important than I was. What it meant was she would never be home anymore to play with me or care for me when I got ill. It was a bribe, a bad one I must say.

Soon after, I was introduced to Ms. Jackson, a live-in mommy replacement my mother hired. I lost Cali that day on the swings and never truly adjusted to the switch.

§

Nurse DeeDee, that's what she told me to call her, visited twice a week for as long as I could remember. I saw more of her and Ms. Jackson than of Mother. I don't have much to say about Nurse DeeDee besides I thought she was a vampire. She consistently wanted to poke my arm for this reason and that reason and took lots of my blood away with her.

Ugh, I thought, *this lady likes to drink me.* Well, at least, that's what my imagination led me to think. Nurse DeeDee was also a strange-talking vampire, constantly referring to viral loads and CD4 counts. I never wanted to see her coming and was extremely thrilled to see her go.

It was an ordinary day when I saw Daddy pull-up into our driveway. Daddy did stuff like that. He'd pop up unexpectedly to take me shopping or out to a movie. The movies were fun because I'd pretend I couldn't see the screen, and he would hold me in his lap the entire time to make sure I didn't miss anything. Before the show began I would drill Daddy with questions my mother never had time to answer.

"Daddy, why is Momma so afraid to let me go outside and play?"

Responding in a nurturing tone he'd say, "Because you are a special little girl, Princess."

"Why does Mommy come home so late at night?"

"Because she works all the time, sweetie, to provide for you."

"Why is Nurse DeeDee so thirsty? I think she likes to drink my blood."

He looked at me in amazement as he chuckled and said, "No, honey, she isn't drinking your blood. She's there to help you."

"Help me do what?" I made a quick comeback, but I

knew the look Daddy would get when he just couldn't find or didn't want to find the right words to tell me.

"Eat your popcorn, Princess. The movie is about to start."

Daddy peered at the screen and I took my normal two-hour nap on his lap. I hardly ever made it past the previews before I was out like a light, no matter what time of the day it was.

But this day when Daddy showed up at our door was different. He didn't come to take me out for the day; he came to take me forever. Daddy called me down to the living room and asked if I would like to move into his condo with him. I still remember jumping on his lap screaming, "Yes, yes!"

My daddy held me tight and said, "Well, Princess, get your things. You're coming with me."

Running so fast, I tripped on the first two stairs, caught my balance on the third one, and raced to the top. Not knowing what to grab first, I shouted over the banister into the living room, "Dad, can I take my Tickle Me Elmo? I like the way he laughs."

"Yes, Princess, you can take whatever you like," he said calmly and patiently. The conversation going on in the kitchen between Dad and Ms. Jackson I could barely hear, and I really didn't care to hear it anyways. I was leaving the den.

"What time is Mommy coming home? I want to tell her bye," I shouted again.

"I don't think she's coming home tonight, Tasha. She's away on business. I'm coming up to help you pack."

When Daddy started packing *all of my things,* I thought, "Wow, I'm really leaving. This isn't a grab-your-overnight-bag type of trip, I'm really moving away. No more nannies, cold cuts, or big ugly kids next door." As Daddy continued packing, I wondered about lots of things, especially if the move meant no more Nurse DeeDee.

During my daydream, I thought back to one bright summer morning I decided that I had had enough of Nurse DeeDee poking me and I would play a trick on her. I figured if I made my arm slippery, she could not stick me and take my blood away. Quickly, I snatched the large tube of Vaseline Mother kept underneath the sink and stuck my little hand way down to the bottom of the jar. It took some force to pull my hand from the glob; my fingers were all stuck together. Enthusiastically, I smeared it on both arms like jelly just as the doorbell rang. Ms. Jackson greeted

DeeDee.

"Tasha, Nurse DeeDee is here, honey," I heard her say.

"Okay," I shouted. "Me will be right there," I replied, as I pretended to act innocent and nice.

Nurse DeeDee performed her normal vampire rituals getting glass jars and tubes all lined up on a blue cloth she placed on the table. Quickly flicking the light switch in the bathroom and leaving a greasy film on everything I touched, I sprinted down the stairs and headed to the kitchen. "Will this be long?" I pouted. "I don't feel well."

"Hey, Tasha, sweetheart," she spoke quietly, "no, we won't be long. Are you ready?"

Any other time I would be far from ready and Nurse DeeDee would be forced to reach into her bag of tricks to persuade me. She kept a batch of stickers you could scratch and sniff that let off an aroma that enticed you to lick it. Or she'd give me a tube of lip-gloss that smelled so good I did lick it. But that day all I wanted was a good laugh. I couldn't wait to see her put on those white plastic gloves and watch them slip and slide all over the place. I didn't want to give her anymore of my blood. To my surprise, she never even bothered asking me about the slime. With a few alcohol pads, she cleaned the area to be pricked, gripped my arm a little tighter than usual, and the blood flowed from my body into her vampire tube—she did it again.

§

"Tasha, sweetheart, what are you daydreaming about?" I heard my daddy say from across the room. "Did you get everything you want in here? If not, we can always come back."

"Huh?" I remember saying. I had drifted off into la-la land and forgot we were packing and I was moving away.

3 BEST FRIENDS FOREVER

The move went pretty smooth. When Mom and Dad split, Dad bought a two-bedroom condo in Chicago and I always had my own room there. It was small and cozy, not an overflow of toys I never played with, but stocked with books and electronics. The floors were hardwood so Daddy bought me a plush, pink carpet to cover the exposed areas. My closet was average. I glanced inside and saw many new outfits hanging.

"Ah, this dress is cute," I said. I knew it was new by the tag dangling from the sleeve. Daddy always bought me something new before a visit, but this time, there were lots of hanging tags. That was a clear sign I would be living with Daddy indefinitely. The best part of my room was the large window with a view of the neighbor's backyard. It was my favorite part of the house because that's where I first saw Jamia. "Dad, can I go play with that girl over there?" I knew he wouldn't disapprove because I would be within eye-sight.

"Sure, go play but be careful."

"Okay . . . I love you," I shouted, as I sprinted towards my jacket.

"Tasha, wait a minute honey, come here." I walked back to the living room and Dad quizzed me.

"You remember our secret, right?"

"Yes."

"Okay honey, I trust you, and I know you will do a great job."

"Bye," I shouted, dashing out the door. When I reached my backyard, I saw this skinny little girl with short ponytails. Her skin was on the brighter side of the African American color scheme, and she already had boobies. I thought to myself, *she has to be older, but I don't care. I've never had a real friend before.* Moving slowly toward the gate that divided us, I waved my hand nervously.

"Hi, I'm Tasha," I said with my forehead pressed against the fence. "Can I come play in your yard?"

"Hey, girl, I don't care." I waited a second to see if she

would look at me like the kids did at my mothers' house but she didn't. Happier than I'd ever been in my life, I skipped through my gangway to the front of her house and through the backyard.

"What's your name?" I quizzed.

"Jamia."

"How old are you?" I had to ask. I wanted to know how old I might be when I started to grow boobies.

"Nine."

"Oh, I'm eight. Where's your mom," My questions kept rolling.

"Inside. Where's yours?" I didn't know how to answer that, hadn't seen my mom in over two weeks. She was away on business, so I blurted out, "I live with my dad."

"Oh, that's sweet," Jamia replied. "Why do you live with your dad?"

"Cuz' my mom always at work and I get sick a lot, so Dad wanted me to be safe."

"What's wrong with you?"

"I don't know; something wrong with my blood."

Daddy and I practiced that answer time and time again, and that was the first time I actually got to use it on someone.

"Why are you out here by yourself?"

"I have to get away from my mother sometimes because she's crazy."

I looked at her and laughed. *I guess all moms are crazy,* I assumed.

"Are you going to transfer to my school?" Jamia said.

"I guess so. Daddy says I'm here to stay, and my mom's place is far, real f-a-r."

It was like love at first sight. I knew Jamia would be my friend forever. We played in the backyard for the rest of the day, and by the time I went inside, all I could do was think about what tomorrow would bring for my new BFF and me.

§

That summer was the best summer of my life. Jamia and I would walk to the candy store for pickles and pop. She seemed to enjoy having a protégé, and I liked having a sister. Jamia quickly learned all my favorite foods and we liked all the same music. But best of all, she knew the look I'd have on my face when I wasn't feeling well and would sit with me while I was sick. That little girl had all the qualities I only wished my mom had, and as the days grew, so did my love for her.

One day we ran into the living room where Daddy was watching football and jumped on the couch with him, one on each side.

"Mr. Davis, is Tasha going to my school this year? I really want her to," Jamia exclaimed.

"Yes! Nice play. That's the way you do it," Dad shouted at the screen. "I'm sorry, girls, what were you saying?"

It was obvious Dad couldn't concentrate on two things at once. "Never mind, we'll come back later. Come on, Jamia, let's go to my room." I understood game time was never a good opportunity to throw serious questions at Dad because I wouldn't have his undivided attention. We usually used game time to ask for money because he'd reach down in his pocket and hand it right over.

As soon as we made it back to my room Jamia announced, "be right back. I gotta' pee."

"Ugh you nasty" I joked. Mia took off.

Minutes later she arrived from the bathroom with a bottle of meds in her hand. "So, this is what makes you sick, Tasha?"

"Wait, what are you doing with that," I yelled.

35

"It was left out on the sink in the bathroom."

"You shouldn't be touching that, Jamia, it's mine." I could see her trying to read the bottle, but we were both far too young to understand it. I fiercely snatched it from her hand and scolded her for invading my privacy.

"I'm sorry, Tasha, jeez. Don't kill me over it."

Jamia had no idea of all the education I had about my meds. *Tasha, you need to take this every day in order to grow big and strong. Tasha, if you ever forget to take this you may get very, very sick. Tasha, these meds keeps your heart pumping and blood flowing, you understand?* So the thought of Jamia breaking the bottle and losing one caused me anxiety and sparked an awkward rest of the day for us. But we made it through it.

When the game was over, Daddy crept into my room. "Yes, Jamia, she will be going to your school. Will you look after her and treat her just as well as you do here at home?"

"Uh-huh. I won't let anything happen to her, Mr. Davis," Jamia spurted.

As he made a sharp pivot out of the room we turned our heads slowly toward one another, stuck out our tongues at the same time, and screamed, "*AHHHHHHH.*"

4 NEW SCHOOL AND CURIOSITIES

Jamia was a year ahead of me, but our playground and recess spot was the same. The only difference was our lunchtime. I hardly ever ate anyhow so that didn't really matter. The food made me nauseous. My classmates began to ask why I spent so much time in the nurse's office, and as their curiosity grew, so did my temper.

Tyrone was the class clown, from what I heard, in second, third, and the fourth grade. It became obvious it would be him that would receive my wrath one day. By the fourth grade, interest about my disease grew a lot, and the old baby talk wasn't working for me anymore. I didn't care about healthy bones and pumping hearts. I wanted to know why I was the only person who had to be extra careful when all the other kids played freely. I saw teeth get loosened at school, knees scraped and bruised in gym, and even witnessed a boy get poked so hard with a pencil that he bled. I wanted to know why I was excluded from certain activities and was tired of the hush-hush.

Mommy came to pick me up most weekends after I moved in with Daddy. When we were alone, I took the opportunity to ask questions about everything. "Mom, what is wrong with my blood? Please tell me." The look on her face after that question was never pleasant; in fact, it looked painful.

"The same thing that's wrong with Mommy's and Daddy's blood, honey."

"Well, what's wrong with your blood," I asked impatiently.

"It has impurities in it that other people's blood doesn't have, Tasha, sweetheart. Now can we talk about something else?"

Now what the heck is that supposed to mean, I thought. She wants to talk about something else after she used the word "impurities. No she didn't" I hated when she ended conversations. It always had to be her way, and I was never satisfied with her answers. But what my parents didn't understand was that I could read. For some reason, they never saw me as a blooming girl that would learn to read and comprehend. In fact, finding out what the word *impurities* meant was promptly added to my to-do list.

It all came to a head one day in the school library when the librarian offered us free time and I chose the computer. I wanted to find a children's site on the disease and learn just how bad this blood thing was.

A quirky little page popped up, and I read the words *Terminal Illness. Terminal* had been one of my spelling words, and I knew what it meant—ending, fatal. But as I scrolled down the page, the biggest shock hit me. It read, most people born with it won't live to adulthood.

My chest began to close up. It felt like all the air had been sucked out of the room and my breathing spun out of control. I don't remember screaming, but Tyrone made sure I didn't forget it. He was the first to run over to my chair, pointing and shouting, "Something is wrong with the crazy girl, something is wrong with the crazy girl."

I cried hysterically. One thing was for sure; I didn't forget to exit that page. I couldn't bear to know if someone else saw what I was reading. Who knows what came over me, but in an instant I pounced on Tyrone. I hit him in the face, kicked, bit, and cursed him. "You son of a bitch, I'm sick of you."

"Let me go you crazy girl, let me go," Tyrone squealed.

With each scream, I clutched his throat harder, trying to make him eat the words he shouted at me. It took both my classroom teacher and the librarian to pry us apart. If my looks could kill Tyrone would be dead but if Ms. Stewarts look could kill, I'd be the one six-feet under.

The look on my teacher's face was unforgettable. She stared at the large knot growing on the side of Tyrone's head. She looked even more disheartened when she saw blood dripping from my lip. Ms. Stewart sprinted anxiously to the front office for help, trying to stay calm, mumbling, "bring gloves."

In the meantime, everyone else was warned not to touch me. I was devastated—never felt so isolated in my life. Attacked by the class clown and not one person seemed concerned with him, concerned only with the drops of blood that trickled down my chin.

By the time the nurse made it to the library, I had already walked out of the room toward her office. I heard someone behind me. "Tasha, honey, please wait a minute," the nurse called.

"Why, what am I waiting for? To die," I responded. She said she couldn't believe how grown-up I was acting, but the world would never know that being grown-up was all I knew how to do.

When the nurse finally caught up with me, I'd already wiped the blood from my mouth with the sleeve of my shirt and simply wanted to run away and hide.

"What happened in there, sweetheart?"

I tuned her out, something I learned to do very well with my mother. The only word I could find was "daddy."

"Would you like for me to call your father?" the nurse asked.

"Yes," I replied and burst out into tears. It felt like I had cried for hours by the time my daddy made it to the school, but only one had passed. After hearing his heavy footsteps in the hall, the intensity increased and I cried even louder. It was such a relief to see him.

"Tasha, honey, I came right away. What happened?"

I tried to talk, but jumble, slob, and bubbles were the only things escaping my mouth.

"What happened to her?" he questioned the nurse.

"Mr. Davis, calm down, please. I've been trying to get the whole story myself, but Tasha hasn't been feeling up to telling me yet."

Daddy held my chin in his large hand and looked at my face. I could feel the heat rising underneath his skin as he examined my swollen lip.

"Do you mean to tell me someone hit her in her mouth, and you're sitting here like you don't know what the hell happened? Get the principal in here and her teacher— NOW! I need answers right away," he demanded.

I stopped crying long enough to tell him that talking to anyone wouldn't be necessary. All I wanted to do was go home. Daddy observed me speechless, took my small hand in his, and we stormed out of the nurse's office and into the parking lot. He opened my door, and I got in. He stared blankly at the school doors before climbing in the car himself. As he reached for his seatbelt I said, "Daddy, can you get Jamia an early dismissal, too?"

"Tasha, I can't just take other folks' kids from school without their parents' permission."

"Her mom is crazy. She won't care." A look of disappointment came over his face.

"I'll try to call first. It's only right, but don't let me hear you call her crazy again. That isn't nice."

"Okay."

Daddy marched back into the school building like a decorated officer. I was frightened to know what type of chaos he would cause inside, but what worried me far more was thinking about what might happen the next day at school. There was no way I would allow any teasing of me about being a Daddy's girl and I surely wasn't going to have anyone mocking me about the incident in the library. My mind was made up that I would fight every day and everyone if I had to. No one would make me feel bad ever again, I promised myself. But at that moment, I could care less about the other kids. I wanted to kill Tyrone.

From the looks of things, Jamia's mom agreed and out they came. Mia jolted out of the school doors bouncing around like crazy, swinging her arms up and down as she marched to the car unaware of the trouble I had.

"Dang, girl, what's the deal with pops taking us home early?" Mia asked as she put on lip-gloss using a tiny mirror, never looking me in the face.

"I had a fight. We'll talk later," I tried to say before Daddy got in the car.

Her neck almost popped off when she snapped her head in my direction. "WHAT? With who?" I gave her the eye. Mia caught on instantly.

The ride home was as quiet as a library on a Saturday night. I knew Daddy was furious, but we understood each other very well. He never allowed his pain or hurt to overshadow mine. Looking back now, my father was the type of guy most women would call a real man. He never wanted to do anything to upset me, even if he felt otherwise. I truly loved my papa. He was a true Hero.

VICTIM IMPACT PANEL

I had to pause for a moment because remembering my dad like that made me extremely emotional, and tears welled up in my eyes. "I'm sorry. I haven't talked about my father to anyone lately, and I'm, well . . ." The audience was extremely attentive.

I continued . . .

By the time we made it home, my head was pounding, stomach sour, and I was scared to death. Jamia followed me to my room, and Daddy strolled to the fridge to grab a beer. I remember him not looking so healthy, but back then I was too young to understand what was really going on.

"What happened at school today, sis?" Jamia asked like she would burst if she held it in any longer.

"Mia, I'm dying," I blurted. In that moment, I was about to break my first and only promise to my father and mother and share my ugly secret with someone other than them or my doctors.

"What do you mean you're dying?" she asked as a huge tear traveled down her left cheek bone.

"I read on the Internet today that people born with my disease die before adulthood."

"What do you have, Tasha? I don't understand."

I heard my father walking around and thought the coast was clear so I tried to whisper to her really low and fast.

"I have—"

Right then, Daddy pushed the door open and peeked inside. "Are you girls alright?"

"Yes," we answered in unison.

"Wanna' go out for ice cream?"

I said no, but Jamia's confused face said enough for me to change my mind.

"Well, get your shoes then, and let's go."

I was in no mood for ice cream, but that was what Daddy did for us when we felt bad. It was pretty normal. We went to 31 Flavors on Madison Street, and I ordered three scoops of sherbet while Jamia had a mint double-decker sugar cone. Daddy ordered coffee. The ice cream settled my stomach, and by the time I finished it, I actually felt a little better.

"Girls, when we get back to the house, I want Jamia to go home, and, Tasha, you need to take a nice warm bath and get some rest. I have some work to do, and can't be distracted."

"Okay," we said, again, at the same time. Jamia and I were together so much we were becoming one.

Looking back, I now understand why Daddy stopped me from telling Jamia about my status. He feared our relationship would change if she knew the truth. He feared telling me the whole truth. And now I know he feared the fate of his own future as well, and that was something he never spoke about back then. I never told Daddy what really happened at school that day because I also feared what he might have done to Tyrone. That was one of the times where all I wanted to do was talk to a friend and really unburden my soul.

5 BLOSSOMING WOMEN

It was beautiful outdoors. Jamia couldn't have asked for a better day for her eighth-grade commencement ceremony. Only her BFF was sicker than usual. She was leaving me behind for a year, but that morning, I felt horrible, and it wasn't because I would be left behind. It was hard for me to focus and concentrate. Perched on the toilet, elbows pressed deep into my knees, I thought; *if I can only make it through the ceremony Jamia would understand if I couldn't hang out afterward.* Besides, she was spending a lot of time with our other neighbor, Triston, anyhow.

Jamia and Triston dated secretly. She knew her mom would overreact if she found out about the relationship because Mrs. Bolden was a teenage mother. The slightest moves Mia made were always attributed to being fast and sexually active, so she made sure to keep her relationship hidden.

Triston was a freshman in high school already, one year older than Jamia, two older than me. He was a jokester, always trying to find the greatest punch lines of all times. He was a cute boy, not the best, but cute. His mother dressed him well, and he kept money in his pocket. Often times I caught him staring at me through the corner of his eyes. He made it easy to question if Mia told him I had a disease. Or even easier to believe he was a slick dude hitting on me low-key.

I trusted Jamia with all my heart and she never betrayed me before or told my secret to anyone, so I placed Tris in the whore category as a default. I categorized him as such because if Shay, another girl from school, hadn't told me that I was a very pretty girl, it would be hard to believe. Before her, Dad was the only person to tell me I was pretty. When I looked in the mirror, I only saw bumps, scars, medicine bottles, needles, and rubber gloves—never a gorgeous seventh grader. But, in Triston's defense, maybe a pretty girl was all he saw and he wasn't a whore at all.

Right in the middle of my thoughts, still atop of the

toilet, I felt a dizzy spell come over me combined with severe stomach cramps. Then suddenly, bile erupted from within, leaving sticky green ooze on parts of my lap and all over the floor. The room began to spin, and at that very moment I was struck with the worst case of diarrhea one could ever imagine.

This can't be happening, not on Jamia's big day. I've been sick lots of times, hospitalized more than you could imagine, but never, ever, on Jamia's birthday, and I surely can't miss her one and only eight-grade graduation, I worried. There was a tap at the door.

"Honey, are you okay in there?" Daddy questioned.

"I'm fine," I played it off. "I just need to shower, and I'll be ready to rock and roll. I can clean up this mess, too. No worries."

"Are you sure, sweetheart?" Daddy said.

"Yes, Dad, I can make it," I said irritated. Daddy knew I didn't like being treated any differently than other kids. It was upsetting to think of differences all the time. I wanted to be normal, like everyone else.

I glanced at the mirror on the wall next to the toilet and saw the mess. My face was a mess, hair was a mess, and I made a nasty mess on the floor. I wept in silence. Sliding my body over the bathtub, one leg at a time, I turned the water on high to conceal the sounds of my pain.

Jamia crept inside the bathroom. Funny how the aching pain altered my senses because I never noticed the door open up or her sneak in. When I finally realized someone was in the bathroom with me, I peeped from behind the curtain, squinting my eyes at the foggy mirrors. I saw Jamia on all fours, with tears in her eyes, cleaning the mess I'd made.

Through my embarrassment, I pretended not to see her and started singing as if everything was okay. Deep inside, I knew she didn't buy the singing-in-the-shower performance. Jamia understood I was really sick but to prideful to let her down.

The stench of vomit blended mixed in with the smell of peach shower gel and Clorox bathroom cleaner made me nauseous all over again. Soon, I found myself back on the toilet with sweat beads forming on my forehead as I pushed in pain. You could say I was drifting in and out of consciousness because I could smell the cucumbers mom planted in her garden, saw the kids playing from the big picture window in living room, and then I pictured the old trusty swing set she bought me.

How could Daddy cater to me so much and Jamia learn my every desire and my own mother knew nothing about me? I whimpered in silence, afraid that Daddy might insist I stay home. Why was Mia there cleaning my bodily fluids, and my mother was somewhere living the good life? I was in pain, physically and emotionally, and needed to gather up enough energy to take a second shower.

It wasn't easy, but I finally made it out of the bathroom without another incident. Snatching the Pepto-Bismol from the medicine cabinet and drinking some straight from the bottle, I yelled, "Get out of my room, guys. I'm coming in to get dressed." I knew Daddy and Jamia would be in there waiting to see my face so they both could tell me how it was okay if I stayed behind. But I refused to let them pity me. To my surprise, they were already gone. Being wrong wasn't a bad thing especially when it was at the expense of my feelings being spared.

Sitting on my bed I could see Triston leaving the back gate toward the front of the building. He was going with us to the ceremony. Laughing out loud a little, I wondered if his friends teased him for dating a girl in grammar school. That made my day. I dressed as fast as I possibly could and headed to the door.

We loaded the car, waiting patiently for Jamia's mother to come down. Going outside was a task for her. It felt weird in the car with Mrs. Bolden because she never left her apartment. I found out later that she, too, had a disorder. She was schizophrenic and agoraphobic. I finally understood what Jamia meant when she said her mom was crazy.

§

My stomach cramped the entire ride and for most of the ceremony. Just as Jamia was called across the stage, it hit me. A pain so vulgar I couldn't resist bending over, resting my head in my lap, while squeezing my stomach with both hands. After it eased up a little, I nicely but urgently asked the guy next to me to move so I could exit the section. It would have been horrible if I accidently ruined his nice brown suit. I ran to the bathroom in barely enough time to pull up my dress. My body felt like it was emptying beneath me. My head thumped, and the room twirled and danced about dizzily. Eventually I was able to move again, literally dragging my own body out of the small stall, and then I slouched over the sink to clean up. I was gone so long Jamia came looking for me after she marched out of the auditorium and found me slumped over the bathroom sink, with hardly enough energy to move.

"I couldn't miss your graduation, but I need to go to the hospital. I feel like crap," I finally admitted.

"I love you, Tasha . . . You didn't have to do this for me," Jamia cried as she slung one of my arms over her neck and eased the weight of my body onto her shoulders.

We made our way into the hall. "I have her, Mr. Davis," she said to my dad who stood guard right outside the bathroom door. He looked like he would have barged in there if we would have taken just another minute longer. "Can you please go get the car?" Jamia asked, as we walked toward the exit. My daddy picked me up; gently placing me across the backseat of the car, then closed the door.

I heard Jamia tell him, "Mr. Davis, I'll be at the hospital later. My family is waiting for me in the lobby ready to take me out to lunch. Please don't question Tasha about this; she is in a lot of pain."

"Sure thing, Mia. Thanks for helping, and being such a good friend to her."

Jamia opened the back door where I was stretched across the seat, leaned in, and kissed my forehead. "Love you, girl," she said softly.

"Love you, too, Mia."

She turned her back to me and faced where her mom was standing. "Ma, do you want to go with me or go home?"

"Home. I've had more than I can take."

"Aunt Viv, can you and Uncle Ron take my mother home for me? Triston and I will meet you at the restaurant?"

"No problem, kiddo," said Aunt Viv as she looked down at me. "Tasha, you get well, and we will see you next time, oaky, honey?"

"Okay," I mumbled, as Daddy drove away.

I threw up twice more before arriving at the doors of the hospital where a triage nurse, who of course, knew me by name, was there to greet me.

"So, Tasha, you're not feeling well today?"

"No, I feel like shit, excuse my language." In fact, I was ready to have a pity party with a slew of *why-me* questions to throw at any receiving ear. I just wanted to have a normal life, just for one day, and couldn't. I wanted to go out and have lunch with my friends, I wanted to like boys, I wanted to tell secrets to my friends, but I couldn't. I wanted to throw things around that damn hospital, but I couldn't. I wanted to know what the fuck was the big-ass secret that Daddy refuses to talk about. I wanted my mother, but I didn't have that either. Again, right in the middle of the triage area, I broke down. I knew I would be admitted, but this time, I vowed to ask as many questions as I could to educate myself about my illness. After all, I was going into the eighth grade, so it was time I took matters into my own hands. I lived with Daddy since end of second grade, and he *still* treated me like a second grader.

I had had enough.

6 EIGHTH GRADE BLUES AND NEWS

I walked in the front of the building feeling lonely.
Jamia and Triston were in high school, and I was left
behind. Of course I had no desire to make new friends.
Teaching myself that people didn't like me wasn't a
difficult task. Being ignored all the time by the other kids
helped me to make that decision. To them, I was the weirdo
of the school. Then, as if my day couldn't get any worse, I
found out Tyrone was in my classroom.

Aw, snap, I thought. *Not this boy again. I promise I
will hurt his ass real bad if he fucks with me this year.* I
wasn't for none of it that time. My new meds were working
wonders and the strength I had was enough to take that fool
Tyrone down if I had to.

Mrs. Anderson was our teacher, and she was a

bombshell. Her nose was thick, but well proportioned. Her top lip had a cute little curve that sat perfectly underneath her nose complemented by a set of gleaming white teeth. Her hips were curvy, hair cut in a short style, and a booty that popped out at you. She wore elaborate clothes with matching scarves and bags all the time. Mrs. Anderson became my idol. I studied her movements and wanted to be sophisticated just like her.

I wondered if she was sick, I wondered who else in the classroom held a deep dark secret. Who had been molested, who ran away from home, or who had a secret crush on one of their cousins. I wondered all types of things, but never, ever, asked anyone anything out of fear of them asking something about me. But Mrs. Anderson changed all that. She gave me something else to focus on besides the dark stuff. She prompted me to work toward a complete makeover. I had the money; Daddy would buy me whatever I wanted.

Eighth-grade year I saw the nurse every Tuesday and went to an advanced reading class. This particular Tuesday was no different besides Tyrone being promoted into my reading group. I cringed when I saw him walk toward me, his long skinny body strolling across the floor.

"Tasha can I ask you something?" he asked sincerely, while I ignored his existence.

"Please, I've been building the nerve to approach you since fourth grade. All I need is a couple seconds."

"Hurry up and spit it the hell out, Tyrone. I wannna' finish this assignment before the bell rings," I said in the most annoyed voice possible.

"I'm sorry for what happened in the library when we were little. I didn't mean to hurt your feelings. I was such an annoying little kid. I never did that to anyone else and would never do it again. Can you find it in your heart to forgive a brother?"

Glancing up at his sad puppy-dog face I said, "No way will I ever forgive you. Now is this conversation over?"

"Tasha—"

"Tasha NOTHING! You humiliated me in front of our entire class," I raised my voice a notch to signal my rising temperament.

". . . but *fourth* grade? I was a stupid little kid back then."

"And now you're a stupid big kid to think a simple apology could make up for what you did to me that day. I was mature then, and it's not my fault you weren't."

"And it isn't your fault that you had to grow up so fast either, Tasha," he stated, overstepping his boundaries a bit.

By the time I looked up from my period of ignoring him, he was sitting in his seat reading the chapter we were assigned. All of a sudden I saw a handsome young man instead of a mean little jerk. At that moment, my heart felt something I couldn't describe.

I couldn't wait to get home from school to tell Jamia everything. When she walked through the door my mouth ran rapidly.

"Girl, guess who approached me today at school," I said with so much enthusiasm Jamia was all ears. "Tyrone!" I shouted before she could even answer the question.

"Tyrone you had to beat down in the library in fourth-grade Tyrone? Are you serious," she roared.

"Yeah, girl . . . He stepped to me all apologetic in reading class today. I couldn't believe that fool."

"I know, right? I thought you'd kill him back then."

"Naw, girl. But he seems different now. Sincere. But I still rejected his apology. He hurt me bad back then, as if I wasn't going through enough."

"True. But how was he to know that? Doubt if he read

minds."

"Whatever . . ." I replied, as I thought about her comment at the same time. "Anyway, moving right along, are you going to the doctor with me this afternoon? I could really use the company."

"Yeah, Tasha, but . . ."

"Uh-oh, here comes the but . . ."

"I promised Triston I'd hang out with him, too. Can he come along?"

"If he doesn't mind waiting in the lobby when I'm called to the back. You know I want you to go to the back with me."

"Sure thang, boo, sure thang. He can wait."

We giggled and buried our heads in our books; it was study time.

Ring, ring . . .

It never failed. As soon as I began to really get interested in my assignments the phone would ring.

"H-e-l-l-o," I said annoyed.

"Hey, Tasha, it's your mother. How are you?"

"Fine."

"How's school going?"

"Fine."

"Are you coming for our weekend visit this week? I missed you the last three weeks because you were so busy."

"Yeah, sure, Mom, I'm coming." Before I could control myself, my sarcasm invaded my speech. "Will you make my favorite dinner when I come?" I knew dang on well Mom had no idea what that was.

"Sure, honey," she replied. "Tell me what it is again and I'll serve it right up."

"Hot dogs and French fries," came rushing from my mouth.

"Then that's what we'll have. Hot dogs and French fries," she repeated.

I hated hot dogs, and that was how she made it easy for me to hate her. She couldn't even remember simple things about me. I don't think my mother ever saw me eat a hot dog in my life. In an effort to cease the dead-end conversation I asked, "What time will you be here Friday?"

"I'm picking you up from school. I have a surprise for you."

"Okay. Well, I'll see you Friday," I said real short and snappy like.

"I love you, Tasha, I really do."

"OK, Mom, I know. Love you, too. Bye."

Jamia and I looked at each other. I didn't have to utter one word. She already knew that I felt—nothing but abandonment from my mom. She hugged me as I thought. I understood we we're all sick, but I was tired of the secrets, the lies, and the sweeping of things under the rug. I was tired of it all.

7 DOCTOR DOOMSDAY

My mind was made up. I would ask all types of questions at the doctor's office that day, but I wasn't sure I wanted Jamia to know all of the details. Triston coming along to the hospital with us turned out to be a good thing. Mia could stay in the lobby with him while I went back.

We had fun on the way there. It was Triston's junior year in high school, and his mother bought him a cute little sports car. "Put on your seat belts, ladies. Let your driver get you to your destination safely. This is your captain speaking," Triston joked while fidgeting with his own belt.

"So are you a pilot or driver? You can't be both," Jamia said jokingly.

"Don't be a killjoy, lil girl. I'm your captain, too!"

We all erupted in laughter. This is how the ride was all

the way to the hospital, joke after joke, and laugh after laugh.

It felt so good that I began to reconsider digging into the depths of my illness as Triston and Jamia engaged in their own personal conversation in the front seat. I wasn't a baby anymore. I knew from school what I had was a sexually transmitted disease, and I knew it resulted in death and also knew it compromised my immune system. But the truth was, I didn't even know what an immune system did or how it functioned. One growing virgin was all I was, nothing more, and nothing less.

Anger grew inside of me. Why would my parents have me if they knew they were positive? Why would they want to put me through this, especially Mom? If she knew she wasn't the nurturing type, the always-there-to-pick-me-up-type of mother, why would she go through with the pregnancy? I needed my mother, didn't she know that? She was being downright selfish.

Tears were rolling down my face when I realized I had killed the mood in the car. "I'm sorry, guys. I just got a little scared about my appointment. I didn't mean to bring everybody down."

"No problem, Tasha," Triston said. "Hey what's wrong

with you anyway?"

Jamia slapped the side of his arm. "Boy, you shouldn't ask personal question like that."

His eyes bulged bold and confused like.

"No, Mia, it's cool. I can handle this," I said. "Tris, I have a rare blood disease that I don't even know much about, but today is the day I begin to ask questions."

"Oh, sorry if I offended you, but Jamia loves you to death and a friend of my baby is a friend of mine."

"Thanks though but, I'm good,"

"No doubt," he replied

Now the car was dripping with silence. No one said a word, and for the first time ever, I was glad to see the hospital parking lot. I wasn't up for winging answers to anymore questions I didn't know the answers to.

We walked into the hospital, and a chill met us at the door. I gestured for both of them to have a seat in the waiting area while I marched to the registration desk chewing bubble gum.

Checking in was a no brainier. I'd done it so much I never read anything anymore, just sign, sign, sign. My father and I submitted waivers that stated he didn't have to be present for routine visits anymore, which made me somewhat happy. The older I got, the more and more uncomfortable it became to answer certain questions with him staring in my face.

Politely handing the clipboard to the receptionist, I sneezed. "I'm sorry," I said instantly at the same time she said, "bless you."

"Thank you," I replied, while placing the clipboard on the desk in front of her. Something told me to glance back at her. I did. The ignorant receptionist had her face all screwed up in disgust as she grabbed a disinfecting cloth to wipe down her desk.

How unprofessional, I thought. She was already ugly, no need for the ugly face. I guess she figured what I had could be passed on through a sneeze. Deciding to ignore her ignorance because I had enough on mind, I hopped in the seat next to Jamia.

"Girl, how long is it going to be today?" Jamia asked.

"I don't know, chica. What's on the stupid tube?"

"*Jerry Springer.*"

"Cool . . ."

I needed some laughter. The questions I was prepared to ask the doctor were weighted. Unsure of how I'd feel afterward, laughter would be good right now, I thought silently.

From the sliding glass window the nurse said, "Tasha, you can come to the back."

"Wow, that was the shortest lobby time ever. Be back, guys. Don't miss me too much," I joked with them.

"Sure you don't want me to go with you, sis?"

"I'm sure. Be back in no time. Wish me luck." They both threw their hands in the air with a thumbs-up.

I followed the nurse to my room, the old stinky patient room I hated. Those pictures on the wall of unborn babies in the birth canal were quite unpleasant. I hated remembering myself that way, legs bent like a chicken and sick in the womb. Staring hard at the pictures of the stages of pregnancy, I tried to figure out what fetal stage I was in when the virus attacked my body in my mother's belly. I reluctantly pictured Mom and Dad having sex knowing they were sick when they created me—and nausea arrived instantly. I had forgiven my parents for what they'd done to me, but it never took away my curiosity. There was a rap at the door, and my doctor glided in with her nice white jacket.

"Hey, Tasha, how are you today?" she asked.

"O-K."

"I hear your medicine is working out for you this time; no stomach cramps, no light-headedness or diarrhea."

"Nope," I replied. "Um, Dr. James, can I . . ." My words cut off by a fear bubble expanding in my gut. I was afraid to know the truth, but it was killing me on the inside not to ask.

"Yes, Tasha, what is it, sweetie?" I sat frozen. "I'm your doctor. You can ask me anything you want. I'm here to help."

"Never mind . . ."

"Are you sure? I know you're a growing young lady and should be exploding with questions."

"Yeah, but . . . Well, Dr. James, I should be getting my period soon from what my friend Jamia told me, and I don't know what to do."

"Don't you fret; there's something I wanted to talk to you about as well."

Relief set in like a medically treated headache. I was eager to hear our next step.

§

Dr. James thought it would be a good idea to resume

therapy. Daddy stopped taking me when I moved in with him. He reckoned I was far too young to be worried or concerned about things I could not change. I remember hearing my dad tell the old therapist, "I am paying for top-notch medical care for Tasha. She will see a therapist when she wants to and not any moment sooner." Daddy believed talking about my illness would only make me depressed and fearful. He didn't want me to know more than I could handle for my age. But my doctor felt differently. She thought it was time, and I agreed with her one hundred percent.

"Tasha, Dr. Green will be the one you can confide in about anything, medical or social. The one you call on when you feel high or low . . . like a new best friend. Don't worry about her judging or treating you differently from anything you tell her," Dr. James said sincerely. "Do you want that?"

"YES! Would love it. When do I go?"

"Today. It was prearranged. And by the way . . ." Dr. James went on to tell me all about my menstrual cycle and a few other things a young girl should know. She finished my medical examination and handed me a piece of paper with Dr. Green's office number on it. I went right there without telling Mia or Tris a thing.

§

Dr. Green's office was cute. She had decorative rainfalls in the waiting area I absolutely loved. Water always had a soothing effect on me. Nervously I introduced myself to the receptionist. My hand was a little wobbly as I handed off my waiver form so she wouldn't ask for a parent. The young-looking woman with glasses verified the form, made two copies, taped one to a manila folder with my name on it, and put the other one in a file cabinet. Then she told me to come to the back. I walked in with a sense of urgency; I wanted to see my new BFF.

Dr. Green wasn't as beautiful as Mrs. Anderson, my teacher, but she was pretty in her own right. She, too, wore glasses and her hair in a perfect bun. Her outfit was plain, but her warm personality captivated me instantly. By the way she spoke to me I knew I would love her, and she was just the person I needed in my life, a confidante.

After writing a few things on a smooth leather-looking tablet, she looked up at me and said, "Hi, Tasha, I've heard a lot about you from Dr. James, but I want to hear all about you from you. That would make me happy. Are you okay with that?"

"Yes, ma'am," I replied.

"Well, since you're new, I'll start. My name is Dr. Green. I'm not a medical doctor. I'm here to help you heal emotionally and mentally. Anything we say in this room will never leave, alright?"

"Yes, ma'am," I replied again.

The doctor told me about her thirteenth birthday, when her dog died and about a new dog she bought two days ago. I had such a great time in the beginning and found her Q&A's to be something I could handle. By the end of the session, a trusting relationship had developed. I never got around to asking any of my important questions, but I had every Friday afternoon for one hour to work my way toward that. My trip to the doctor turned out not to be so bad after all. Just as I was standing up, reaching besides me to pick up my purse from the arm of the chair, Dr. Green stopped me.

"One more thing, Tasha. Before you go. Are you sexually active," she inquired.

"No, ma'am, I'm not." She scribbled a few more notes on her tablet, stood up, and shook my hand. "Well, I'll see you next week."

I walked out of the office feeling a new sense of self. *I'm sick, but there is still light up ahead—I can feel it,* I thought. Surprisingly, I called Mom before entering the elevator. I wanted to tell her I was seeing a therapist again.

Don't ask me why.

8 WEEKEND AT MOTHER'S

My mother was excited to hear from me and thrilled I was seeing a therapist. When she heard from a little birdie named Mia that there was no school the next day, she shot at the opportunity. "Can I pick you up a day early," she asked. I agreed.

That's how it was with Mom. I always knew she loved me, but as I matured, things were clearer. Mom just didn't know how to love me the way I needed her to.

She picked me up the next morning at 9:00 A.M. Not only was she punctual, but she was an early bird too.

"Hey, Cali," I said. I heard laughter as she walked toward me to help with my bags.

"Don't 'hey, Cali' me, young lady," she chuckled. Mom knew when I called her Cali I was implying I missed her in some way.

"Hey, Tasha," she said as she planted a kiss on my forehead. "I'm so glad you didn't flake out on me, Daddy's

Girl."

"I wanted to, cause I'm gonna miss Mia, but I thought it'd be nice to check up on ya."

"Thanks, sweetie."

Normally I would pop in the ear buds to my headphones immediately to tune her out. But that time they stayed packed away because we clowned with each other on the ride. As soon as we left the city limits we stopped at Dairy Queen for ice cream. When we arrived at the house, there was a strange man standing on the porch waving at me.

"Mom, who is that guy looking all corny and whatnot," I asked.

"Oh, that's Dr. Beech. We became friends over the years."

"Friends, eh? Is that all?"

"Yes, chile, just friends. I don't think I can ever love another man like I loved your father."

That was the most shocking news I had ever heard in my life. The parents I knew didn't love each other. In fact, I remember seeing my mother throw a shoe, hitting Daddy in the head once before. It was a house shoe, but a shoe nevertheless.

"Wow, Mom, Glad you told me that. Good to know."

"Sweetheart, you're getting older, and there's a great deal more you'll learn. Just be patient but try to understand all the choices your father and I made were to better your life. Okay?"

"Yes, ma'am."

We got out of the car and headed to the house. It was still stupid big and appeared even bigger now that I was gone.

"Mom," I said, but there was no answer. "M-O-M, where did you go that fast?"

The house was silent. I crept up the stairs. There was a crack in my bedroom door so I pushed on it slowly to make sure no one was in there. Out jumped Dr. Beech and Mom shouting, "Surprise!" Mother redecorated my entire room, and it was absolutely fabulous. She took an old picture of Mia and I playing in the sand and had it hand painted and framed. My bed was now a huge circle with a perfectly handcrafted quilt clinging tightly to its sides. I couldn't believe it. For the first time in my life Mom had gotten everything right. If Dr. Beech had anything to do with her trying to figure out who I was, I loved him already.

"*That's* what's up, Mom, thank you!" I happily

exclaimed. "And thank you too, Dr. Beech."

Mom didn't reply. She just hugged me tightly. With my ears pressed into her chest I could faintly hear Dr. Beech say, "No problem, kiddo."

They bustled out of the room to let me get acquainted with my new space and settle in. I opened the closet door to put my bags inside, and there were gift boxes on the floor. Kneeling down slowly, I snatched the first box, ripped the paper off, and inside was a BlackBerry Storm. Screaming "THANK YOU" at the top of my lungs as I opened the second box, I could hear my mother giggling. The second box was a brand-new Coach Signature purse. I was in total shock. It was like Mom found my diary and read all the awful things I wrote about her and wanted to make it right between us. Jamia was going to freak out when she saw all my new stuff. I opened the final box and was overwhelmed with joy. The card inside read:

Friends are forever, if you work at it
Friends are like teachers, if you learn from them
But friends should never, ever be forgotten so please
give these gifts to your friend.

I didn't understand at first, but when I opened the box all the way, I saw that Mom bought Jamia identical gifts. We both owned BlackBerrys' and Coach bags. I almost fainted. When I pushed the power button to call Mia, her number was already stored in the phone under BFF, but it rang and rang. No one answered. I was going to burst if I couldn't share the surprise with her.

The crinkled gift-wrap and presents were scattered on the floor when I sprang up to find my mother who disappeared again. I heard noises on the back patio, peeled open the doors, and "Surprise!" rang out again. This time there were more voices. There stood Mia, Tris, my mother, Dr. Beech, Dr. Green, and TYRONE. I was taken aback that Tyrone was there, but I knew Mia was behind that one. I greeted each person individually and the miniature party began.

"So, Jamia, girl, you knew all along, huh?"

"Yep."

"Tris, how come you didn't blab this one? You tell everything else."

"I would have told your peanut head butt, but Mia didn't tell me until today. She knows I'm the bean spiller, secret killer."

My belly filled with laughter. As I conversed with my guest Tyrone blurted out, "And I'm here because you can't keep a good jerk down." We all laughed heavily, and I thanked him for coming and being a good sport. I was the happiest kid alive that day and for the duration of my stay at Mother's.

The weekend went smooth. I would miss Mom. She really outdid herself that time. But I was ready to get home to Daddy because I missed him, too.

9 WHAT'S WRONG WITH DADDY

Mom brought me home a little late. She knew Dad
would worry so I called from my new cell phone to give
him a heads-up. He didn't answer. I left a message. When
we got there all I could see was darkness in our condo.
There wasn't a light on in sight. Mom asked if I could
manage.

"Oh yeah, I'm good," I told her as I snatched my bags
from the trunk and strolled to the door. My key was buried
deep in my pocket. I waved at Mom once I finally opened
the door and went inside.

"Dad, are you here?" I called out, turning the light on
in every room I entered. It was obvious Dad was not home,
and that was abnormal for him. I went to the kitchen to get
a drink of water and saw a note on the fridge.

Tasha, I'm not feeling well. Going to the doctor, be back soon.

I couldn't determine when the letter was written because I'd been gone since Thursday, but from the looks of things, he'd been gone just as long. Sitting at the table, fumbling with my phone case, I dialed Mom's number to ask for her help, but she didn't answer. Too tired from my weekend to worry, I went into the living room to sit beside the house phone and crashed on the sofa. It was morning when I heard the alarm blaring in my ear. Time to get ready for school and Daddy still wasn't home. Frantically, I called Mom again. She answered.

"Mom, Dad isn't here and hasn't been here all night. He left a note on the fridge that said he wasn't feeling well and was going to the doctor. What should I do?"

"Breathe, girl. I can barely make out what you're saying you're talking so fast." Mom calmed me down and told me to go on to school and she would handle everything. So I did—but worried all day about it. He was all that I had prior to my mom's flawless weekend visit, and I was concerned. The worrying crushed my appetite, so I skipped lunch and wandered the halls all period.

"Tasha, get to class," the guard said.

"It's my lunch period."

"Then go to lunch," he said sternly.

As I reluctantly headed toward the cafeteria I thought about how frail my dad had been getting over the last few years and how he never, ever, went to see doctors. For some reason I could not figure out how Dad had the disease but never saw a doctor, especially knowing how much I'd gone to them and been hospitalized in the past. It became urgent that I spoke with my mother immediatley.

My cell phone was tucked away nicely in my new purse. I didn't want it to be confiscated by a bossy school authority figure. Instead, I shuffled to the counselor's office and asked to use the desk phone to call my mom.

"It's an emergency," I exclaimed.

Office personnel were used to my emergencies. They didn't even look twice. Propping the phone between my ear and a hunched shoulder, I reached for a pencil just in case my mother needed me to take notes. The phone rang only twice before she picked up.

"Mom, have you talked to Dad?" I asked.

"Yes, honey. I'm picking you up from school in an hour," she replied.

"Is everything OK?" I was already crying before she

could answer my question. Mom never picked me up from school and that's how I knew something was wrong.

"Your father is sick. We'll talk on the way to the hospital. But, sweetheart, listen, everything will be just fine. Try to focus on your final hour."

She lost me. "Okay, Mom, see you soon." I hung up repressing my scream. That was a complete waste of time telling me not to worry. I loved my daddy dearly. My mind went blank. The hour rolled by. Finally, Mom was in the front parked in her shining new Mercedes. And I ran and jumped in. "I don't want to talk. Let's go."

Daddy wasn't at my hospital, and I didn't like it one bit. The hospital he was in had torn, colored tape on the floor with arrows pointing north, east, south, and west. There were a few homely looking people sitting in worn down chairs. They were watching a fat worn-out TV with squiggly lines that was bolted down to an equally worn desk. I didn't want my daddy in a place like that; he deserved to be treated with class. The sight disturbed me. My mother never uttered a word, but I wondered what she was thinking. It was because of my daddy that she did so well for herself.

She thought I didn't know that when she and Daddy

split, he gave her everything so I could live happily—did it without a fight. He didn't know then I would end up living with him. However, he never, ever harped on it. In all honesty, he actually seemed happy that he helped Mom. I remembered when Daddy told me how he begged my mother to stay with us and she said no took off. He told me Mom said repeatedly that, "she couldn't live a lie." Daddy said he understood and would never stop loving her. Snapping out of deep thought I turned to my mother and shouted, "What are you hiding?"

"Tone it down, young lady. Out of nowhere you start shouting," she said confused. "What do you mean?"

"Why did you leave Daddy?"

"Sweetheart, this isn't the time or place for this. Your father is sick, and he needs us right now. We can have this talk later."

"Later, later, it's always later . . ."

"I guess you'd rather be selfish and make this about you? Huh, Tasha?"

Although, she had a lot of nerve calling me selfish, I figured she was right. There was no need for me to be mad at her now, not when Daddy was stuck in that dreadful place. I sat in silence until we were given our nametags and visiting instructions, but it still did not take away my interest.

Daddy was in a room with three other people. Dingy-looking curtains separated the four bed and he looked frail and helpless. I ran to his side and held his hand tightly while staring at the tube in his nose that made it hard for him to speak.

"Hey, Tasha, honey, I missed you," he expressed.

"I missed you, too, Daddy. What's wrong?" He looked away from me, right past Mother and closed his eyes.

"I'm going to be fine. I have pneumonia, but the doctor says it's clearing up."

My father was a strong man. He would never want us to see him that way, so I refrained from asking questions that would challenge his strength. A doctor walked in and gestured for my mother to follow him into the hall. I assumed, *just some more damn secrets.* I peeped out of the room and could see my mother's head bobbing up and down in response to whatever the doctor told her. I saw them shake hands and Mother wipe a tear from her eye before reentering the room. That was when I realized Daddy's grip on my hand loosened. When I turned toward him to see why, in the blink of an eye, he had drifted off to sleep.

"Kiss him good-bye, Tasha. The doctor said he needs his rest."

I asked her if I could have some alone time with Daddy, and mom left.

"Dad, I know you can hear me. I love you and need you to come home," I whispered softly into his ear before leaving his room.

"OK, Mom, spit it out. What did the doctor say?"

"That your father is in there fighting for his life. He isn't out of the woods yet, but if he keeps fighting hard, he could survive this bout of pneumonia."

"What else? What about the HIV? Why don't you ever tell me anything about that?" I was annoyed, frustrated, and hurting. I was sick and tired of the lies and deceit. Mother was about to see a side of me she didn't know existed if she told one more lie out of her mouth.

"Tasha, honey, sit down on the bench. Let me share some things with you.

Your father and I were the happiest couple alive until the disease hit us. My life was destroyed, our lives were destroyed, and I couldn't cope. But your father remained to be the loving person I've always known him to be. He sold his property left to him by his parents, drew down his entire retirement plan, and gave it all to us; he also gave me the down payment for my business that for some reason God has blessed tenfold. But I don't know why he refused treatment, Tasha. I can't even begin to tell you why he didn't seek proper medical attention for himself, but made sure you and I were well taken care.

I have talked to him often about the disease not being a death sentence. He knows I wanted nothing more than for him to start medical treatment. But I assure you; I had absolutely nothing to do with his decision to decline help. I am just as confused as you are.

You want to know more about your illness? I understood that before you ever mentioned it to me. I'm your mother; I know these things. It was me that contacted Dr. James to request therapy for you again. I was a girl your age once, and I saw how you looked at Tyrone the other day, too. You like him, don't you?"

"Yes," I smiled shyly, "but this is about Dad—Please don't try to change the subject."

"After those goo-goo eyes you laid on him that day in the backyard, I was glad I stepped on your daddy's toes a little because he will always see you as a little girl, and hiding information from you at a crucial time like this would be a bad thing to do."

"M-O-M, you're pushing me. I want to know about Daddy – Not Tyrone."

Pushing my bangs from my face Mother said, "So trust me for once, can you do that for me, honey? Just trust me for once?"

It couldn't hurt to give her a chance. What else could happen? Besides, at that moment, I needed any comfort I could get.

That day I agreed to trust my mother's judgment and value it a little more than in the past. We held each other in an affectionate embrace on the hospital bench. Something happened that day between Mother and me. I felt like we were becoming a family again.

10 LUNCH WITH TYRONE

Raschida and Tachell were my new lunch buddies when Mia left. They were a couple of girls I liked all along but never gave them the time of day when Jamia was around. We sat eating awkwardly when I saw Tyrone cruising to our table with his lunch tray.

"What's up, y'all?"

"What's up?" we said together.

"Ty, why are you cutting class? Don't you have lunch next period?" I quizzed.

"Nope, I got lunch this period."

"How?"

"Don't worry about all that. Are you glad I can bring some excitement to this lame table?"

We giggled, and I gently pinched the side of his arm. Tyrone was right, though; the chatter among the group grew when he arrived because he cracked jokes on everyone in the lunchroom. No one was safe.

"Look at David over there with that big ole do-whoop forehead. For real, though, look at Michelle thinking she cute in those red Levis," Tyrone joked. We laughed our jaws off at who wore last year's coat and who had the nicest hair. We talked about graduation and the last dance. I waited anxiously for Ty to invite me in front of the other girls, but, of course, he was too macho for that. The bell rang and lunch was over.

"That was the shortest 50 minutes all year," Ty yelled.

"Wait, before you say it . . ." I looked Ty dead in his eyes. "I know what you were about to say. Lunch went fast because you were here. Am I right?" I questioned, looking at Ty with a smirk.

"You know me so well! All hail to the king of 6th period lunch."

Rashida and Tachell smirked at each other, reacting to our corny inside joke. We picked up our trays and marched to the trash in a single-file line, Ty behind me. That was the first time I didn't want school to end. I wanted to sit in the cafeteria forever. Lunch went on like that every day, the four of us talking and trading "yo' mama jokes."

One day someone brought up sex and lunch period was intense. Raschida and Tachell claimed to be virgins like me, but word around the school was Raschida had been around the block already, at 13. I never wanted to believe it, but her language was much too vivid not to have experienced some of it on her own. All of a sudden I could hear Daddy, *"Please don't tell our secret. It will turn your best friend into your worst enemy, that's just how the world goes."* Why that popped up in my mind, I would never know because I had no intention of ever revealing my secret to anyone else but Jamia. The fear I felt about the topic could be unbearable at times. I tried dreadfully not to think of people finding out. I asked, "Hey, guys, when you do start juicing, will you get tested for diseases often?"

"Girl, why are you asking that?" Raschida was first to respond. "Don't you think I would look at the person first and know if they're good or not?"

"No, no, better yet, why are you calling it juicing?" Ty interjected. "It's getting busy . . ."

Giggling, I said to Raschida first, "Girl, you can't look at a person and know if they're sick. And Ty, getting busy, juicing, making love, having sex, whatever . . ."

Looking like she was about to blow up if she couldn't get her next word out, Raschida shouted, "BS I can't! They will be all bumpy and stanky and stuff like that—you know, looking all wack."

"*Shh,*" the rest of us said together not wanting our cover blown that we were having grown folk talk at our kiddie table.

I was baffled at the ignorance I was hearing that day. They were looking right in my face, a regular little girl (so they thought). If they knew what sick looked like, I would have been put on the spot right then because kids are cruel—everyone knows it. Tyrone taught me that back in fourth grade.

"Well," Raschida said, "I don't think I would want to know anyhow. It's kinda scary." The table fell deadly quiet for a moment. "Anyway, on another note, Tasha, don't forget my birthday party Saturday night. It goes down at my parties."

"OK, Raschida. I'll think about it. You know I don't know anyone."

"You're good, girl. You're cute. It won't take long to warm up and meet people."

"Cool."

Back in class, my concentration was at an all-time low. *How could people be so simpleminded to think illness was a visual thing? In some cases it is,* I thought, *but not all.*

"*Tasha . . . Tasha,*" Mrs. Anderson called from the front of the room. "It's your turn to read." There was nothing I could do then but focus and recite the words on the page. Since I tuned out the previous readers, I had no idea what the story was about anymore, so I read mindlessly.

By the time the 2:30 bell rang, I was mentally exhausted. I thought of nothing but how some people viewed illness and how others could be so shallow. Why did I have to grow up so quick? I couldn't help but wonder if I'd be just like them if it wasn't for experience. Therapy day couldn't come fast enough. I wanted to see my new BFF, Dr. Green. We had a lot to cover in an hour. But first, I had to get up the nerve to go to Raschida's party. I knew it would be awkward, but I needed some good old-fashioned fun.

11 MY FIRST PARTY

Daddy was finally home from the hospital and looked stronger than the last time we saw each other. I appreciated him now more than ever. The thought of losing him did me bad.

I had three shirts on the bed as potentials for the party and one on as I scurried over to where he was seated.

"Dad, do you like this pink blouse?"

I spun around so he could get the full effect. Daddy looked at me in awe like he often did.

"Yeah," he replied. "It's nice for a birthday party—appropriate."

"OK, then it's settled. I'll wear the blue one instead."

Daddy laughed in amusement. He knew I started to hate his taste two years ago, which meant pink ruffle dresses were out. However, I believed he was on to me. He would pick the one he didn't like, knowing I would choose the opposite. That was Daddy for ya.'

Someone knocked on the door just as I got into the shower. I knew it was Jamia because she knocked and twisted the knob at the same time.

"Hey, girl, you can wait in my room. I'll be out in a minute," I shouted from the bathroom. I missed her. Since Jamia graduated, we saw a little less and less of each other, but she was still my best friend. In one hour I could catch her up on a month's worth of gossip. I had to; Jamia was the only girl I totally trusted.

"So you're going to Raschida's party, huh?" Jamia exclaimed.

"Yep. Can you believe it? Thought I'd never open up to new people."

"I'm glad you are. And look at you, sis, looking all cute and stuff. Is your booty getting bigger, girl?"

"Stop it," I laughed it off but was really serious. "You know I don't like to see myself like that."

"Like what? Cute? Sexy? Hot?" Jamia said laughing.

"I guess." We snickered and kept it moving.

Jamia was checking out my outfit making sure my accessories were in order and shoes weren't wack. She was indeed my sister. She knew how much that party meant to me. The only party I'd ever gone to was hers, no dances, no park district hangouts, nothing. The most I'd done with other children were school field trips and it was time I experienced life a little.

"So, Mia, you're still dropping me off and picking me up, right?" I whispered in a very low voice.

"Well, that was another reason I came by so early. Tris has practice, so he can't drive us."

"Oh . . . w-o-w . . . so I can't go?" I said disappointed. "You know Daddy's still sick and can't drive me, right?"

"Yeah, girl, you're going. I wouldn't have you miss this for the world. I'm taking you on the bus. I ain't shamed. Are you?" Jamia was hilarious and always, always knew how to make my day.

"No, I ain't ashamed—thank you. And thank you for being the best friend a girl could ever ask for." Looking in the mirror at the completed outfit, I was ready for my big adventure.

§

The party was a blast, and when Jamia and Tris picked me up afterward, my mouth ran a mile a minute. "That was one of the best nights of my life. I met a few new people and finally had more phone numbers to store in my new phone.

"Was Ty there?" Mia asked.

"Yes, and . . . and we danced and talked and . . ." I dominated the conversation all the way home.

§

A few days passed by and life was perfect. School was going great and lunchtime was a riot every day. One day after lunch, Raschida and I were walking to our art history class when we noticed something sticking out from underneath her locker.

"Wait, let me run and see what that is," she said. I stood still waiting, but had a clear view of her as she jogged down the hall to her locker. It was some type of note. It was hard to make out Chida's facial expression, but I could tell she was reading something. Suddenly, she balled it up and hung her head low for a moment before punching a dent in the locker. I ran toward her. Just as I got closer, Chida tried to toss the note in the trash can.

"No, wait, Chida . . . What did it say?" I asked.

"Nothing to worry about; just someone being a bitch."

"No, let me see it. We're in this together. I consider

you my friend."

Raschida handed me the balled up piece of paper, and my heart hurt for her. It read: *You are one nasty little slut. Your party was nothing more than a whorehouse. I hope you have mono, too, like everyone else, you filthy slut!*

I was confused. Who has mono? I wondered. I knew it was said that Raschida had been around, but what did they mean they hope she caught mono, too? I hugged her, and we went to the bathroom to figure some things out.

"Are you cool, Chida?" I questioned.

"I'm cool. You know, Tasha, I'm not a good girl like you, but I'm not a bad girl, either, and I can't seem to shake this reputation." I let her keep talking since this was the first time she opened up. "You remember Brian from seventh grade, right?"

"Yeah."

"Well, I slept with him before he transferred because I thought we were in love, but that bastard told the entire school about it, and I haven't been able to live it down ever since."

"I didn't know that."

"I know, because like I said, you're a good girl. You hung out with Jamia all last year, and no one else, so you probably cared less about rumors."

"Were there others, too?" I asked.

"Others what?"

"Other boys you juiced, I mean, slept with?"

"No. That was it. One time and one time only, but no one believes me."

"I believe you, Chida. Please don't cry. Trust me, we all have secrets." And as those words escaped my mouth, I saw exactly what could happen if the school knew my secret, especially since Raschida was my girl now.

There wasn't really much I could say. Her feelings were hurt, and I'm pretty sure the entire school was gossiping about it. All I could do was stay with her until she felt confident enough to proceed with her day. But as if things weren't bad enough, we heard through the intercom system, *"Raschida Williams, please report to the main office; Raschida Williams, please report to the main office."* We both knew that something big was going on. "I'll go with you, don't worry," I said. "Let's go get to the bottom of this." Raschida didn't say a word and we marched like soldiers directly to the main office.

"Good morning, ladies," said the clerk at the desk. "Raschida, Dr. Jones would like to speak with you in private. Tasha, I'll give you a pass back to your classroom." I didn't want to fuss about it so I took the pass and told Chida I would catch up with her later. That was another long day where I drifted in and out of social awareness. I couldn't wait until the final bell to meet Raschida at her locker, but that time never came. Later on, I got word that her mother picked her up shortly after her meeting with Principal Jones. No one seemed to know if she was suspended or what. Whatever was going on, I was sure to find out.

When school was dismissed, I pulled my cell from my bag and dialed Raschida's number.

"Hello . . . this you, Chida?"

"Yep, what's up, girl?"

"Nothing. I've been worried sick about you. What happened? Why did you go home?"

"It's a long story. Can you come over?"

"I'll ask Mia and Tris for a ride but can't promise you anything. Are you in any trouble?"

"No, I'm embarrassed a little, but not in trouble. I'll tell you all about it when you get here. I gotta go now."

"OK, I'll try to see you later."

Of course, the next call made was to Mia, but she

didn't answer. I left a message.

By the time I got home, Jamia was there already watching TV, and Daddy was in the kitchen looking like his bill of health had been wiped clean and he was given a new start.

"It's nice to see you looking so well, Daddy. I missed seeing you whipping up snacks in the kitchen."

"Hey, baby girl, how was your day?" he replied.

"Um . . . OK, I guess."

"That doesn't sound good. Anything I can do? You know I have no problem coming up there to straighten things out."

I laughed. "No, Dad, everything is fine. Just girl stuff."

"OK," he said. "Girl Stuff . . . I'll leave t-h-a-t one alone." That was our cue to run into my bedroom and close the door.

"Do you have Triston's car?" I asked.

"Yeah, chile, what's up? We need to roll out or something?" Mia was always in a joking mood. I guess Tris was rubbing off on her.

"Yep!" I said seriously. "I'll tell you all about it in the car."

We had to be extra careful because dad would flip if he

knew Mia was driving illegally since she was underage. But ever since Tris taught her to drive, it was on. That was another one of our many secrets we kept with each other.

On the ride, I filled Mia in on everything, the note under Chida's locker, the call to the principal's office, and her sudden early dismissal from school. Mia sat in amazement listening to my story and was just as anxious as I to get to Chida's house. As we pulled onto her block, I called Raschida to let her know we were there. She gave me strict instructions to ring the bell and act like I randomly dropped by. She didn't want her mom to think she had been gossiping about the events because she warned her of how quickly drama could escalate. Mia pushed the button, we stepped back, and waited patiently on the porch.

"Who is it?" I heard Ms. Williams say on the other side of the door.

"Tasha," I responded, as the door bolts clanked and clicked.

"Hey, Tasha, come on in. Nice to see you. How's your father doing? Raschida told me he's been really sick and in the hospital."

"Oh, he's much better, Mrs. Williams. Actually, he

was up cooking right before we left. You've met my sister Jamia, haven't you?"

"No, I haven't, but I've heard a lot about her. It's nice to meet you, Jamia. You girls can go ahead upstairs. Raschida's in her room."

Knock, Knock, Knock.

"Come in, y'all," she whispered.

"I don't mean to be blunt, Mia," Raschida exclaimed "but you won't tell anyone what I'm about to tell you guys, will you? I've been through enough name dragging for me and you both!"

"Dang, girl, can we get through the door good before you put me on the witness stand?" But anyway, naw, you can trust me. I'm not the one to tell secrets," Mia explained, and I quickly cosigned. "Nope, she's never told any of my secrets." Jamia and I gave each other that look.

Raschida said, "OK, then. I trust you too. I've cried enough, so I guess I can get through this. Jamia, have you ever played Seven Minutes in Heaven?"

"No, but Tasha told me you guys played a few games at your party. Tell me about it."

That was a typical Mia response; she knew I had told her everything about the games we played, but it was her way to keep Chida's trust for me locked down.

"Well," Raschida continued, "it's a silly game of an enhanced version of *Spin the Bottle*. You spin the bottle twice, one for male and one for female. Instead of doing some crazy act right in the middle of the circle, whichever two people the bottle lands on go into the closet for seven minutes together."

"And then what?"

"Well, then, they do whatever they want to in there."

"Whatever like . . . what?" Mia asked concernedly.

"Like . . . um . . . kissing and touching and stuff."

"Did everyone play?" Jamia questioned further.

"Yeah they did, which is why I don't understand how the heat is coming down on me the way it is." Raschida finished her statement with a tear welling up in her left eye socket. "Well, I guess someone had mono and didn't know it, and now several people are home sick with the virus. I was called into the office for questioning, like I murdered someone or something," Chida finished the story in tears.

Like the big sister Mia had always been to me, she wrapped her arms around Chida and told her not to cry, that everything would be OK. With her face flat on Mia's shoulder, wetting up her silk blouse, Chida said in a sniffling voice, "But I didn't even kiss anyone in the closet. I didn't want anyone running around school spreading more stanking-ass rumors about me."

"I believe you, Chida." I blurted out. "It's cool, girl. We're going to high school in a few months and won't see half of these cowards anymore. You don't have mono, and I don't have mono, so what does that say about the rest of them? They were the ones in the closet getting busy and are using your party as an excuse to hurt you, but they messed with the wrong girls this time! They really did!"

Raschida, taking courage, said, "You're right, girl; it's time I fought back."

"True, true. But on a more serious note, Chida, can I ask you something?"

"Sure."

"Do you still believe that you can tell when a person is sick just because they have a bumpy face?"

"No way . . . this right here taught me a lesson. You can't judge a book by its cover, so you're better safe than sorry."

"Amen, sister girl!" I said. "In fact, I'm glad we aren't so scared to talk about serious issues with one another. Now, if only we could get the rest of the world to join us."

The room fell silent. However, in no time, we were all laughing and talking about a plot to get back at the people who had picked on Chida since seventh grade. The main one was a girl named Priscilla. She used to like Brian back then, but he chose Chida. Apparently, she never got over it and it was time for her to pay. I guess after beating Ty down in the library fourth-grade year, no one really wanted to go there with me. But Raschida was my girl now, and I cared a lot for her—we both had a deeper side to us that many people didn't know.

"It was nice meeting you Chida. Don't forget our plan," Mia said as we gathered our jackets and purses to leave. "I gotta get out of here to pick up Triston from practice. He'd freak out if I'm late in his car, thinking something terrible may have happened."

"Thanks, Jamia, for listening. I won't forget the plan," Raschida said as she closed the door behind us.

I thought the ride back would be nothing since all the dirty laundry had been laid out inside, but Jamia was uneasy, I could tell. I knew her.

"What's up, sis? Why the long face?" I asked. Mia looked at me with a concern I hadn't seen before.

"Did you kiss in the damn closet, Tasha, and you're

not telling me? Don't you know that in your condition you could get far sicker than the other kids? Your immune system is already compromised—"

"Wait, wait, wait a minute!" I said, stopping her midsentence. "Are you saying you don't believe my story, Mia? Have I ever lied to you about anything? EVER?" I was pissed at her tone.

"Tasha, I'm just saying. You're sick, and you might be inclined to omit some of the story in fear of what I might say if I knew you were kissing, too."

"Fear who, Mia? What the hell are you really saying, that you would tell people I'm sick?"

"No, I'm not saying I would say anything. What I'm saying is—"

"No, screw it. I don't give a damn about what you're saying. You have officially said enough, and you're starting to sound like my dad."

"Tasha, wait a minute now. Don't get all upset because I'm trying to get to the bottom of this. As your friend, I want to make sure you're taking good care of yourself by not doing risky stuff. I'd die if I lost you to something as simple as a little kiss."

"A simple kiss, huh? What the fuck do you know about

me? What the hell do you know what it feels like to be scared to kiss or fear you may never be kissed because of some awful disease that you didn't ask for? Huh? Answer that question for me. What do you know about anything besides what Tris wants and how he wants it? I'm more than sure you guys are doing way more than kissing—" I was on a roll, but Mia wouldn't let me go off on her like that.

"Wait, Tasha, you're taking this way out of hand."

My perfect gift of tuning people out came into effect immediately and I blocked out every word flowing from Mia's mouth. I was done with that conversation. *How dare she not believe me,* I thought. I was devastated. When the car pulled up to our block, I was anxious to get the heck out of there. I wasn't ignorant enough to slam the car door, but furious enough to shout, "Don't you ever speak to me again," and I stormed into my building.

12 A NEW LIFE

I cried myself to sleep that night after my argument
with Mia; in disbelief she pulled the mom card on me. My
stubbornness set in, and I decided to never share anything
personal with her again. I had determined that she was not
who I thought she was over the years, and I didn't intend to
go back on my decision. I told her everything; we shared it
all, or so I thought, and for her not to believe me was like
the end of the world. I felt like Mia saw me differently, like
a sick kid who would play risky. In no time, I began to feel
ill. I could have never imagined holding grudges could
make me physically sick. But illness fell upon me hard. I
was weak, lost my appetite, and had shortness of breath. So
I went to talk to Daddy.

"Dad, are you awake?"

"Yes, hon, is everything OK?"

"No, I feel sick. Can you take me to the doctor,
please?"

"Sure, honey."

Long ago, Daddy stopped asking if I was sure I needed medical attention because he knew if I asked, I needed it.

Two days I spent in the hospital and not once did I call Jamia to let her know. There was never a time she didn't visit me during my hospital stays. The good side of me said I was overreacting, but something deep in the tissues of my stomach said if I couldn't trust her, then our friendship was done.

The attending doctor didn't understand where the sudden fatigue was coming from because my medication was working well and vitals were all strong. He asked me a series of questions my regular doctor wouldn't have asked before releasing me the next morning. I was relieved. I did not, under any circumstances, want to miss my meeting with Dr. Green, my therapist.

The next morning, I was back home in my bedroom looking out of the window into Mia's yard. I thought about the day we met and how many hopscotch's we'd drawn on the pavement over the years. I knew Daddy had told her I'd been in the hospital, but I didn't care. Daddy broke my thoughts, calling out to me from behind my bedroom door.

"Sweetheart," he said, "can we talk for a moment?"

"I'm really not up to it, Dad."

"I won't take too much of your time.

Dad then eased into my room, sat on the edge of the bed, trying not to invade my personal space. "I just want you to know that your mother loves you very much, as do I. And Jamia loves you like a blood sisters. You know that, don't you," he asked, as I shook my head in a yes motion. "No matter what, don't fall into the trap of not allowing people second chances. I only wished your mother had given me a second chance, but she . . ." dad stopped to clear his throat, "never did and never looked back." I looked at him in amazement. I was shocked to hear him open up about their past as I listened closely.

"I always believed she would come back, but she didn't. I guess what I'm trying to say is, don't give up on the people you love."

"OK, Daddy, I'll keep it in mind. I'm just hurt Mia didn't believe me after all we've been through."

"Understood. But don't let all you've been through go to waste over one bad decision, OK, hon?"

I gave Daddy a hug because we broke a barrier. He'd never spoken to me about his past, and I wanted him to know I would be a great listener if he ever wanted to talk to me again. It was the beginning of another healing process for me. He hugged me back and left my room. Not another word parted his mouth that day.

The doctor said I could return to school in a couple of days, and I knew Raschida wondered where I was so we could proceed with our plan of revenge.

"What's up, y'all? Glad to see me back at our popping lunch period?" I said jokingly as I approached the table after having been gone for a week.

"What's up, chica?" Tachell replied cheerfully. "Where you been?"

"Home taking care of my dad. I think he's off to being a healthy man again." I made that cheap comment, although from the looks of things, Daddy wasn't in tip-top shape.

"That's good."

"So Chell, did Chida fill you in on *the plan* to . . ." Before I could get the rest out Raschida looked at me stern and big-eyed as if no one else was to know the scoop. I caught on quick.

"Like I was saying, *the plan* to thoroughly decorate Ty's locker for his birthday with red and pink Happy

Birthday balloons and embarrass him in front of all his jockey friends? "

"Naw, she didn't tell me, but I'm down."

"Cool, where's Ty anyway?" When I asked that question the table went quiet as ever. No one seemed to want to tell me where Ty was. Secrets, secrets, secrets were the way of life around there.

We talked about our plans for graduation that was coming in a month, what we would wear, and where we would go afterward. The girls were happy to be ending that part of their lives but scared of the next big thing at the same time. It seemed like just yesterday I was living with Mommy, and then moving in with Daddy, and then I was going off to high school. Time flies.

Lunch was over. As I reached for my tray I saw Ty at another table sitting with Priscilla and her crew. *I'll be damn,* I thought to myself, no wonder no one wanted to say where Ty was. Traitor . . . eating with the enemy.

When I got to my locker there was a note stuck in the cracks. Now I pray for the sake of me staying sane that some lowlife isn't trying to criticize me like they did Chida or *I'm going off,* I thought to myself. My hands were fidgeting as I opened the note. To my surprise, it wasn't hate mail; it was an invite to the final dance from Ty. My heart felt warm. I called him after school to accept. Chatting about this and that for about an hour made me almost forget to ask him why he had lunch with Priscilla and them.

"So why were you with them, those ugly girls?"

"Who? Priscilla? Naw, she's cool—you just have to get to know her."

"Oh, OK . . . don't think that will be happening, but have a ball, homey."

Chuckles bellowed through the phone. "Aww, I see . . . Is that a little jealousy I detect in your voice?"

"Jealous? Nope, don't think so, but angry, yes. You know she's very mean to Chida, and I don't appreciate that."

We went back and forth about it a bit longer but the conversation went well, overall. Ty and I decided to color coordinate for the dance. This was going to be epic. I felt it. My first times for everything were happening fast.

VICTIM IMPACT PANEL

I peered over to my left. From the corner of my eye I could see something white fanning in the air. It was the panel facilitator signaling me for a break by waving a piece of paper. Just as I finished my last statement about preparing for the school dance, leaning over towards the microphone and blocking my view, she said, "there will be a fifteen minute intermission."

To me, I figured people would be scurrying out of the room in boredom of my coming-of-age story, but they weren't. In amazement, they wanted to hear the ending. I knew the main reason people filled the room was to hear how a girl like me could be arrested for an act as common and as human as sex. The reality was . . . I was a criminal in the eyes of the public. But I did not forget my purpose and those judging eyes would not deter me.

The break lasted twenty minutes, during which I was

locked in a back room away from the audience. When most people returned to their seats, I was brought back to the platform to communicate what I had done to Ty. Fear sat in once again.

13 GRADUATION PARTY

Weeks passed, and I hadn't heard from Mia and wished she would have called me, but I knew she was hurt by the way I reacted. Life wasn't the same without her, and I needed to apologize. The wound couldn't heal. I called. There was no answer, so I left a message as I gazed out of my bedroom window and into her backyard. "Hey, Mia, it's me. Please call me back when you get this message. I'm really sorry?"

Today was the big day. We would make Priscilla pay for what she did to Chida, so I dialed her up right after I called Mia.

"Hey, girl, you ready?" I asked.

"Yep, I'm good," Chida replied anxiously. "You nervous?"

"Nope."

"Well, let's do this then. I'll see you at school."

For a moment, I started to have second thoughts because I didn't know how Ty would react when he found out I hid behind the bleachers and taped a conversation he had with Priscilla after gym class the week before. I hoped he wouldn't hate me afterward, but Priscilla was a monster, and deserved what she had coming to her.

When I saw Chida, Ty, and Tachell walking toward our table, I felt a little nervous. Chida sat down and gave me the eye which confirmed it was too late to back out so I tried to relax and act normal. The next thing I knew, giggling filled the cafeteria. Faintly in the background, I could hear the recording playing, and each time, it got louder and louder.

"Ty, can I ask you something?" Priscilla's voice was heard in the recording.

"Sure, what's up?" Ty responded.

"Will you go out with me to the dance? You know I can rock the boat like Aaliyah."

"Sorry, Priscilla, I'm going with Tasha."

"Oh . . . OK . . ." she said embarrassed. *"I'll catch you around."*

"We're still cool, right?"

"Yep, we're cool."

The tape played over and over again until all the kids in the room started singing the chorus to Aaliyah's song

119

"*Rock the Boat—Work the Middle.*" I was so engrossed in the fun I didn't realize the gripping glare Ty had on me.

"How did you record that, Tasha? You invaded my privacy!" he shouted.

I didn't know what to say. As I pretended, not so hard I might add, to have empathy for Priscilla, Ty stormed over to her table in front of the entire lunchroom. But before he got one word out, "*POP*" was all you heard. Priscilla had slapped the heck out of him, and they were escorted to the principal's office to keep down any more confusion. Chida and I looked at each other regretfully, and Tachell finally caught on to what happened. She, too, stormed from the table because we left her out of the prank.

All of us got an in-school suspension for the hoax, including Ty and Tachell and were instructed to report immediately. Sitting in the dim cubicle during the suspension was one of the most uncomfortable moments I'd had in a long time. Ty sat right in front of me on the other side of the divider.

"Ty, I'm sorry. I shouldn't have invaded your privacy," I burst out but in a whisper. He didn't respond. It was obvious it would take more than an apology to let him know how sincere I was. Glancing around the room, nervously searching for security that should have been overseeing our in-school suspension, I noticed there was none. I crept quietly out of my seat, slid to the other side of the cubicle, and wrapped my arms around Ty's neck from behind. "I'm sorry, Ty," I said. "Don't be so mad at me. The dance is tomorrow."

He said nothing and sat stiff as a brick. I planted a kiss on the back of his head and crept back to my seat, not wanting to be caught and barred from the dance altogether. We knew one more incident would mean full exclusion, and I didn't want that. After detention, we all silently went in our own separate ways. I was still kind of tickled.

§

The wind was blowing really hard when I got home from school. I knew Mom would be over to pick me up to finish shopping for the dance. Lately we spent a lot of time together. Mom even bought a few things for Ty, but I felt too guilty to tell her what I had done and that he may not be going with me to the dance after all. I didn't even bother going inside the house, thus I sat in the front yard and waited.

"Hey, Tasha," I heard someone say in the distance. I looked around to see where the voice was coming from. It was Mia approaching from behind.

"Hey, Mia," I yelped.

"Your mom couldn't possibly know about our argument because she insisted I come shopping with you guys today."

"It's cool. I'm glad you're here."

"Got your call, too, and I wanted to call back, but hell, for the first time I didn't know what to say to you." It was hard to watch Mia's vulnerable side because she was always the strong one between the two of us. She continued, "Tasha, I will always believe you, no matter what, but I will forever be your protector, too. Do you understand that?"

"I do," I said shamefully.

"Do you remember when your father asked me to look after you when you came to my school? Well, nothing ever changed for me since then. You're the sister my mom never had, and I won't let anything happen to you—EVER!"

It was one of those moments you simply understood, no more words needed to be said. We were snickering and joking in no time as if nothing ever happened.

"Hey, Mom," I shouted as her car pulled up. She rolled down the passenger-side window and hollered, "Come on, girls, let's go SHOPPING!"

Before the day was over, I had everything I needed for the dance, graduation, and the summer. Of course, Mia got her shop on too. It was another day to remember.

"So, Mom, will you be by tomorrow to see me off to my dance?" I asked.

"I sure will, wouldn't miss it for the world."

I stuck my head in the driver's side window and Mom kissed my cheek while Mia grabbed our bags from the trunk. It was sleepover time, we had a lot of catching up to do, and that we did.

I was thrilled to hear Ty's voice that night when he called, although he was very angry with me about the prank. But he forgave me on one condition: "to never betray his trust again." I agreed, and we moved on.

Dance night was perfect. My parents were together in the same room fussing over me, Mia and her mother came by to see us off, and Ty looked extremely handsome. It was only an eighth-grade dance that ended at 9:00 P.M., but it was a feeling I would never forget. It was almost like I was healed.

§

Graduation was the same as the party—PERFECT. Although I did feel a little sick from nervousness, I prayed long and hard for what happened to me at Mia's graduation to not rear its ugly head—and it didn't.

That was the first time I met Ty's mother. She looked stern but gorgeous at the same time. Ms. Johnson didn't say much, but she seemed to be extremely proud of her son. Ty graduated with honors; Salutatorian, perfect attendance, and a science fair recognition. Me on the other hand, I was glad enough to walk the stage due to all the days I missed over the years because of my condition, but it did not reduce my excitement. It was weird though. Throughout the entire ceremony I could think of nothing more than Ty kissing me good night. I replayed that vision over and over in my head for weeks, *my first kiss*. It was fairytale like.

The most we'd done was hold hands in the halls, but we were so shy, that never lasted longer than ten seconds at a time. I looked over at Mama and couldn't help but wonder if she saw the glow in my eyes? I hoped she didn't because I wasn't up for the lecture.

§

"It's over! We're officially high school students now,"
I said to Ty outside, where crowds of families were taking
pictures, and you could lose your group in the mix if you
didn't keep your eyes open.

Balloons were soaring in the air, rose petals adorned
the ground, and I was in bliss. Ms. Johnson said, "Get
closer so I can't take your picture, guys." Ty quickly took
me by the neckline, and we posed for the shot.

My mother yelled, "Wait, wait, I want one, too. Don't
move."

My father was moving kind of slow, but, of course, he
wanted his own shot as well. Mia and Tris stood there
looking on amused with each other. The best way I can
describe that moment was magical

14 HIGH SCHOOL

High school took a toll on me physically, and my peers saw it. Eyebrows were raised when people noticed me struggling to tackle those treacherous stairs, long hallways and carrying my books. For the most part, Ty would carry the books to class for me if our classrooms weren't on opposite sides of the building. I didn't meet a lot of new friends but I was plugged because Tris and Mia had already made their marks.

I missed three weeks of school my first semester. It was then I realized Daddy wasn't doing the best he could. I felt my time with him was limited, so I spent most of it catering to him and talking about any and everything. He told me things I never knew, and we bonded.

"Dad, why won't you get treatment? You know I feel you're being selfish to me by letting yourself go like this," I pleaded with him.

"I talked to a doctor last week."

"You did?" I said excitedly.

"Yeah, I did. We're discussing treatment options now, but I won't make any promises to you. Just hope it's not too late for me to turn things around."

"That's good, Dad, I'm happy for you. What made you change your mind?"

"Graduation."

"What about graduation?"

"I realized I wanted to be here for the next one and the next one . . ." Dad leaned his frail body close to mine and hugged me tighter than ever before. That was the first time I ever saw my daddy actually cry and release more than a single tear. He let it flow. We made it a movie night after he pulled himself together. Dad would finally seek help and it made me feel brand new. I was proud of him. My life was changing for the better.

Mia was over every day after school when I was sick. She kept an eye on Ty for me, but never had an ill word to say about him. Mia thought he was the perfect gentleman. It made me happy to be his girl. He was one hunk of a guy, great personality, smart, and had a huge loving heart; he could have any girl he wanted, but he dealt with little sick me.

"So, Mia, has Tris applied to any schools yet? How did he do on the ACT?"

"Good, girl. He can go wherever he wants. Why'd you ask?"

"Oh, I'm happy for him, and, um . . ."

"Yep, I'm listening. I know there's a *but* coming."

I didn't know how to tell her that I was being selfish like my dad. I knew if Tris went away, and he and Mia were still together, she might consider leaving too, and I didn't know if I would be able to survive another separation from her. In the midst of my thoughts, I heard Mia cough and say, "Spit it out, girl, I'm listening."

"Mia, I know if he leaves the state, you would leave with him the next year, and I don't want you to." The look on her face was one of shock.

"Now why would I do that?"

"Cause you're in love."

"True. But Tris knows my circumstances."

"I hope you don't, Mia, cuz I won't have anybody if you do."

"What about Ty and Chida?"

"Chida's been hanging with other girls lately." Mia hadn't really paid attention to Chida's actions because she was too busy keeping a watchful eye on Tris and Ty. But I noticed it all. Chida and I would always be cool, but high school had a greater variety of people to choose from, and I didn't make the cut. But Mia knew why I needed her. She was the only person who understood me; she was the only person I could be 100 percent truthful with. I just wished for the best and never, ever considered the worst.

Back at school, I had a lot of catching up to do, and with Mia's help I did—She did a lot of the work for me. My strength grew each day with a few weak ones every now and then. I continued to eat well and exercise and fall deeper and deeper for Mr. Tyrone.

Mom had been calling a lot lately, and I thought we were good. She wanted me to start going to school from her house a couple days a week; said she didn't mind the drive. I was gaining popularity at school, and things seemed to be looking up. So, I figured, what could two more days away from everyone hurt? I went to Dad's room and he appeared to be sleeping, but as I turned to walk out, "Morning, Tasha, what do you need," he said in his morning voice.

"Nothing, Daddy, I wanted to hang out with you for a minute to tell you what Mom asked me yesterday."

"What? Is it something I want to hear?"

"I don't know about all that dad," I said jokingly. "She wants me to start going to school from her house a couple days out of the week."

"Really? What brought that on?"

"I don't know."

"Well, hon, you know it's up to you. You're in high school now. It's time we start letting you make some decisions on your own."

"Thanks. You're way too cool for me." We exchanged smiles, I kissed his cheek and hurried out so I wouldn't be late.

"Hey, Mia," I said to her when we bumped into each other in the hallway. "Why didn't you wait for me this morning?"

"I met with a chemistry tutor so I don't flunk punk-ass Mr. Bynum's exam. Are we on for this weekend still?" Mia asked.

"That's what I want to talk to you about. Do you know why my mother wants me to hang with her more? Ya know, you seem to get filled in on things before I do."

"Nope, don't know what that's all about. Why? What

did she say?"

"She wants me to come over this weekend and go to school from her house on Mondays and Tuesdays. She even volunteered to drop me off and pick me up."

"Wow."

"Ha, *wow* is right."

"That's cool; quality time with your mom is good, I guess." We laughed again, "Let's just set another date for the sleep over. This should be interesting." We both went to class. Another day was done.

My mother was at my house at 3:00 sharp waiting for me to get home. Things were different this time. Mother was not waiting in her car, which meant she must have been inside. She never waited for me inside. This had to be big. I opened the door, and there sat Mom and Dad having a cordial conversation and it was a relief that I didn't have to witness any arguing or fighting.

"Hey, Mom, hey, Dad, what's up?"

"Nothing," they said together.

"Your mother was just telling me her plans to have you over on Mondays and Tuesdays from now on."

"Oh, that's what's up. Let me go and grab my bags." Something inside of me felt weird so I purposely listened in on their conversation. Unfortunately, it didn't reveal anything other than what they told me. I was shocked.

I kissed Dad on the cheek and told him not to miss me too much. He chuckled. "Bye, Tasha, I'll see you Tuesday. Take good care of her, Cal." Mom gave him a thumbs-up, and we were off to Roselle.

The weekend started off great. We watched movies and caught up on family drama. She filled me in on all the stuff my crazy cousins were doing to their mom and how she was glad to be far away from them at times. But then it all went downhill. Good ole mom began digging into my personal life ranting about how she needs to know more about it. She should have known better than that. We hadn't got to the place where I was with Dad. I had a hard time telling her things because we were never that close, so to ask me out of nowhere, "Tasha, are you thinking about sex?" was totally out of line for her, and I made sure she knew it.

"Don't play with me girl. I'm your mother." It took everything I had in me to keep from saying, "When you want to be." I looked at her, "There's no need to worry. I'm not out having sex. Ty and I have barely hugged, and that's all I can give you right now." I thought I shut her down, but to my surprise, she had a horrible idea.

"Tasha, honey, why don't I come with you to a few of your counseling sessions just so we can start a little unbiased bonding?"

"Wait! What? You want to come . . ."

"Yeah, I think it would be good for us."

"I disagree—"

"I knew you needed help, Tasha. I saw it before your dear daddy would have ever recognized that you were growing up," she said, cutting me off from my last statement.

"Dad hasn't anything to do with this, Mom – please let's not go there tonight."

The conversation was push and pull until I finally agreed to allow her three sessions—that was all. I was just starting to make progress on my own and I didn't need my Mom eavesdropping on my private conversations with Dr. Green. I went to bed early with a lot on my mind.

The next morning, Mom was up making breakfast. The smell danced under my nostrils, and I woke up ready to max. I looked in my purse and noticed my medication was gone. I panicked.

"Mom," I screamed from the top of the stairs, "have you seen my meds?"

"Yes, sweetie, they're down here."

"Why? Better yet, why were you in my purse?"

"Calm down, sweetheart. My doctor called this morning and said that my regimen was working really, well. I wanted to talk to him about yours just to make sure you're getting the best care."

"Mom, stop worrying so much. One thing Daddy did do for you was make sure you had the best, didn't he?" I snarled sarcastically.

She smiled reluctantly with a look in her face like "yeah, right." Mom nodded her head yes and flipped her dark brown pancake.

The weekend dragged, but it was nice being driven to school. Just looking at the scenery made me happy.

"Have a good day, Tasha," Mom said.

"I will and you, too. Thanks, Mom."
Where were Ty and Mia? I needed to vent.

Ty hugged me tightly when he saw me. "I missed you, boo," he said.

"Ah," I giggled. "I missed you, too." We walked to

class hand in hand. It was awesome to have first period with my one of my best friends. "Did you do your homework," I asked him.

"Nope, so I hope you did."

I gave Ty that warm *this can't keep happening* look, but I couldn't lie; it felt good that he trusted me as smart as he was.

"So I saw Tris yesterday. He went to the college fair where I did my community service."

"Oh, really?"

The teacher told us to stop the chattering, but it didn't stop me from wondering about which schools Tris showed interest in. I had always prayed that he considered staying local. My heart told me that Mia loved him so much she would follow him and that would break my heart to pieces.

At the bell, I grabbed Ty's hand and whisked him out of class. "So tell me, what schools did he look at?"

"Too many to remember but most of them were out of state."

My heart dropped to the floor. Ty, obviously, continued to talk from the motion of his lips, but I didn't hear a single word. All I knew was I had to find a way to keep him there in the state, but how in the world would I do that?

Ty went to his next class not knowing I didn't hear a word he said after "out of state," flowed freely from his mouth but he didn't even seem to notice.

15 MOTHER KNOWS BEST

It was that dreaded day. Mother's first of the three counseling session visits we arranged, and things were heated right from the start.

"So, Tasha, tell me why you agreed to have your mother sit in on your session."

I didn't really have an answer for that. I didn't want her there. She was the last person in the world I would want in my personal space like that. So I gave an answer I thought they both wanted to hear, "because she thought it would be good for us."

My mother took the floor, as usual, and gave her reasons for wanting to be there.

"I know Tasha and I have not had the best relationship Dr. Green, and she resents a lot of the choices I made, but I don't want things to continue on that way." They both looked at me as if I was supposed to say something, but I didn't. "Tasha," Mom continued, "has dealt with a hell of a lot, and I never knew how to help her, which made me feel weak and vulnerable."

The room was quiet, tense, and extremely still. This appeared to be an experience of a lifetime. Never before had my mother ever disclosed to me why she let Dad take me without a fight. I wanted to hear more so I sat quietly with my arms folded across my chest.

"When I found out we were positive, my world crumbled. I thought I'd never want to see the light of day. I wanted to be there for Tasha, but I could barely look at myself in the mirror, and I couldn't stand the sight of her dad either."

"Tasha, did you know this?" asked Dr. Green.

"No," I said offering them nothing more to go on than that.

"How do you feel about that, Tasha," Dr. Green wanted to know.

"I don't—"

"Tasha, honey, this won't work if you are unwilling to be open and honest," my mother said.

"What do you want me to say? I feel sorry for you? — because I don't!"

"No, that's not what I want you to say—" my mother

said firmly.

"Well, go on with your story then, I'm all ears."

It was obvious that the meeting was not going so well, and I could see the stern mother I'd always known bursting through. "Tasha, look, give me a chance here. That's always been your problem, thinking you're so damn grown."

"*What?* Are you cursing at me in my session, Mom?"

I couldn't believe her, as if I would open up then. *The nerve of this lady,* I thought to myself. That was the longest hour of my life. I was so glad to see it end and had no desire for next the time to ever happen. But it wasn't over. In the car, my mom felt the need to continue her unwanted rant.

"Tasha, I don't like how you treated me in there. Either you give me a clean slate to work on or I can't work."

"Mom, I gave you that. How can you be mad at me for not showing any emotions? I learned that from you."

"And like I said, whatever you learned from me was the past. I'm asking for a clean place to grow – No grudges."

I listened to her go on in that manner all the way back to the house. Tuesday morning was twelve hours away, and

I couldn't wait for the clock to strike. After that, I didn't have to see Mother again until the following Friday. Trust me, I conjured up in my mind a million better things I could do instead of visiting my mother. I only hoped one of them worked.

As I dressed for school Tuesday, I sat on my bed and stared at the wall. If I were at Dad's, I'd walk over to Mia's and see if she was all ready to go, but I had no friends nearby at Mom's. Mia called just as I was sulking. "Hey, You coming to school today?"

"Yeah, why? What's up?" I replied.

"I need to talk to you."

"Cool. I'll sit with you at lunch."

"All right, see ya later."

"See you later."

Just as I hung up the phone Mom was calling from downstairs. She was ready. *FINALLY.*

The ride to school was quiet. Mom didn't want to rub me the wrong way, and I had had enough of her for the moment. As I exited the car, she said something that struck a serious nerve in my body. "Don't walk around upset all day, Tasha. I didn't mean to hurt you. Now be a big girl."

I was instantly pissed. Being a big girl was all she ever wanted from me, but while talking to Dr. Green, she said I was too damn grown. *Fuck her,* I thought. "Bye, Mom," I screeched.

For some reason, I felt like my own mother was out to get me. I had no faith in her intentions. Jamia, on the other hand always saw the good in Mom. Mia told me how we have to learn to accept people for who they were, and if my mother didn't know how to love me the way I needed her to, that didn't mean she didn't love me. I never let on to Mia that I was thinking Blah, Blah, Blah as she spoke.

We talked so long about my dreadful weekend I forgot it was she who had something to tell me.

"So what's up, chica? What did you want to talk about?"

"You know Tris applied to a lot of colleges, right?"

"Yep . . . so how did it go? Did he get accepted to his top pick?"

"He did."

"Wasn't his first choice Howard?"

"Yep."

"Wow, so Tris is going away?"

"Um huh, and I don't know what I'm going to do

without him."

"I'm still here, Mia. You have me."

That was my way to hint at her promise; it would be her time to apply to schools the next year and I began to worry.

Freshman year was not a breeze for me, but I made it through. My grades weren't stellar, although most kids didn't consider a B average to be bad at all. But something strange was happening to my body. Every time Ty touched me, even if it was a slight brush, I became moist in between my legs. *I'm going to talk with Dr. Green,* I thought, *but I don't want Momma there for that. UGH!* I wished she would have just left me alone.

§

It was Tris's senior year. I had become so popular around school through Tris and Mia's connections that it felt like home on the first day of my sophomore year. It would be an exciting one, to say the least. Mia was going to the prom with Triston and applying to colleges, Dad had agreed to keep taking treatments, and Ty was getting taller and sexier as the years went by.

I dove right into the school year trying to keep my grades high because those sick days had a way of creeping up on me and I liked to keep some cushion. Ty had been hinting at going further, but I managed to brush him off although I didn't know how much longer I'd be able to do that. The three counseling visits with Mom turned into six, seven, eight, and nine. It was frustrating and I didn't necessarily like it, but I did learn a lot about her that I needed to know. One thing I learned was how much she truly loved me. She had a strange way of showing it but, *oh, well*, I figured. We had gotten a bit closer over the summer, but unfortunately we weren't quite there yet. She still knew how to push my buttons.

The really bad part about my Monday, Tuesday visits with Mom, she began leaving me home alone quite often. Apparently, things were getting really serious with her man. I didn't like the feeling of abandonment all over again, but I made up for it another way. Every time she would leave, I would invite Ty over. He would catch the Milwaukee District West Line Train, and I would walk there to meet him. I kinda liked the alone time we had, but the hints of going further turned to heavy touching, and one day he actually put his finger all the way in my vagina and wiggled it around. I never felt so good before in my life. I knew what we were doing was wrong, but somehow, I didn't care.

One night Mom left, we were watching the movie *Harry Potter and the Chamber of Secrets* and just started making out on the couch. He pulled me on top of him, and I rocked back and forth on his lap until my legs started shaking. Ty watched in amazement and clutched my butt even tighter. I won't lie, that was the first time ever I'd been topless in front of a boy. Then the phone rang. It was Mom saying that would be home shortly and that's how that ended. *Saved*, I thought.

I felt horrible. I knew I should have spoken with Dr. Green long before then. Things were spiraling out of control, and I knew I had to do something fast; therefore, I decided I would mention my feelings whether Mom was there or not. Besides, I figured she already had an idea about what I was ready to do. If she didn't say "been there and done that" at least twice a day, it wouldn't have been normal.

§

It was the moment I had dreamt about since last year, my talk with Dr. Green about ways to disclose my status. All types of emotions were built up inside of me. Other teenagers didn't think as hard as I did about losing their virginity; they just did it. Other girls didn't worry as much about losing a dumb boyfriend at my age. If it didn't work out, they merely jumped to the next person and started over. Other girls were normal in my eyes, and I was not. But Ty was my best friend, next to Mia of course, and he deserved to know the truth. But the thought of him leaving me for a healthy girl tore me up inside. I thought so deep that my stomach couldn't bear another minute of it. My belly churned all night long.

The walk from the elevator to Dr. Green's suite, with Mom yapping on her cell phone, was the longest walk ever. I'd walked those halls hundreds of times, but never had I felt so nervous. Dr. Green knew immediately something was different about me, I saw it in her eyes. Boy-oh-boy, I didn't waste any time. The longer I waited to speak, the more frightened I would have become so I blurted it out,

"Ty wants to have sex with me." The look on Mother's face told two stories, one, "I told you so," and the other of "worry."

"Dr. Green, I don't want to be judged or told to wait that I'm too young. What I need are ways to tell Ty the *truth*."

"Well, Tasha—" Dr. Green said, but Mom cut her off with a, "W-E-L-L I am your mother, and it is my job to tell you to wait. Why now? You are only fifteen years old."

"I know how old I am, and this is why I didn't want to tell you. I knew you would judge me."

"I'm not judging you girl, I'm parenting."

"Mom, I know you care about me, but I hope we can get through this. Luckily for you I am sick or we wouldn't even be here in this room in the first place discussing my private life. Most girls I know don't tell their mothers anything – they just do it."

"Well, you're not most girls."

"Go figure," I said to Mom, but I looked directly at Dr. Green awaiting her response.

"Tasha," Dr. Green started again, "this is a big decision you are faced with."

"I know. But can we get on with it please. I was scared

enough to say anything at all."

I could see the uneasiness in her face as she stated, "first off, I want to say I also think you are far too young to consider sex. I am not judging you. I'm only giving my professional, as well as personal opinion." I kept my focus stuck on Dr. Green because from the corner of my eye I could see Mom with a big "I told you so, face" on.

"However, there are plenty of ways to disclose to Ty your status. We can discuss a few of them if you like."

"I would, please."

"One way is to simply tell him the truth."

I looked at her strangely. "I know that. But I guess what I'm trying to ask is, do I *have* to tell him?"

"Yes, Tasha, unfortunately, you do. It is your civil and legal duty to disclose to any potential sex partner that you are positive."

"But why?"

"For one, it becomes a possible threat to your partner's health if the condom comes off, or if he decides he doesn't want to wear one at all."

The meeting wasn't going well. Besides, it got worse by the second because I couldn't keep Mom quiet.

"Look, Tasha, you may not like my approach, but you

better tell him if you know what's good for you," my mother shouted.

"What do you mean if I know what's good for me? Why do you always have to put me down, Mom?"

"I am not putting you down. I'm telling you the truth. You won't do anything but hurt other people if you don't disclose that information. I know that shit all too well."

"There you go with the cursing again. I hate it when you get all dramatic."

The mood thickened between my mother and I and she said some things I don't think I could ever forgive her for. She even looked in my face and said in a disgusted tone, "and you're sitting there looking lost just like your sorry-ass father."

I burst into tears.

"Why does this always have to be about Dad? You make everything into something about Dad. At least he didn't abandon me like you did!" I shouted back at her. That must have struck a nerve with Mom because she started to cry, and I had never, ever seen my mother cry before. Dr. Green sat listening attentively.

"If it wasn't for your father we wouldn't be sick. How's that for your precious dad?"

At first what she said didn't register because I brushed it off like all the other negative comments she made about him in the past. But then it hit, and I said, "What did you say?"

She ignored me. *"What do you mean?"* I cried out. Mother stopped talking, grabbed her purse, and charged straight for the door, but I didn't let her get away. Grabbing her wrist tightly I said again, "What do you mean, MOTHER?"

It was too late to take things back then. She had given up a piece of information I never knew. "Are you saying Dad gave you HIV, Mom?"

"Yes, that's exactly what I'm saying, so stop holding so much against me."

A state of shock covered Dr. Green's face, "Ms. Davis, that wasn't the best way to reveal your secret."

"Why not? She's blamed me every day of her life for leaving. Everything that went wrong was my fault. Whenever I looked in her precious eyes I could have just killed her father. That is the part she never knew. I couldn't pretend to be a happy family, not for her and especially not for him."

I was devastated, but still tried to defend the only

parent I had gotten to know. "That's no excuse, Mom. If you knew you were sick, then why on earth would you have me? You could have adopted if you just had to be a mom that damn bad." I knew what I said was hurtful and uncaused for but my mother had out-done herself, even for Cali.

"T-a-s-h-a . . ." she said, breathing hard and crying intensely, struggling to get her words out, "*you were born a healthy child*. I did not have it during your birth. Your father slept with his slut secretary and contracted it from her when you were only two months old. You got it from my breast milk." Mother broke down, but I am pretty sure a weight was finally lifted from her shoulders.

I could barely breathe. My mind drifted. I could hear Mother crying, and saw Dr. Green jump up to snatch the tissue from her desk, but I wasn't there. It felt so unreal. Not my father, the man who nurtured and cared for me, and treated me like a princess all my life. Not my king of all kings; he wouldn't have done such a thing, but why would my Mother lie? My life was shattered!

Devastation set in like an uncontrolled asthma attack as I looked into Mom's weeping eyes. As far as I was concerned, I no longer had any parents—they were both dead to me. I didn't say anything to Dr. Green either as I grabbed my purse and headed for the door, slamming it so hard a painting fell from the wall in the hall. I don't even remember Mother calling me, but I do recall the long, long walk home. For the first time in my life, I didn't want to talk to Jamia, Ty, and especially not Dad.

He didn't even notice when I came in because he was into his ball game. As I lay in my room, I cried on and off all night.

To hear that news and act normal at school the next day was difficult, but it was surely time for me to be a big girl. There wasn't a soul in the world I wanted to share that part of my life with in that moment. Everyone knew how much I loved my dad.

My purse vibrated all day with back-to-back calls from Mom and several from Dr. Green, but I refused to relive that pain two days in a row. At lunch when I saw Ty's face I wanted to run to him and snuggle in his arms, but I couldn't do that either.

"What's up?" Ty asked. "You don't look so hot."

"Why, thank you, Ty," I said.

"No, really, I didn't mean that to be funny. Can I help you with something?"

"Nope."

He stared at me for a while, and then began talking about chemistry. I didn't want to hear about no damn formulas. Hell, all I wanted was for someone to come up with a formula that would make me well again, like I was as an infant. What I wanted was for my life to not have been a lie. What I needed was some time away from everything and everybody. I stopped Ty right in the middle of his sentence about positive and negative charges and said, "I'm sick, and I need to go home. Would you excuse me?"

"No problem. Let me get your books," he said as he held my hand for me to get up.

"Thanks, we'll talk later." At that moment I realized coming to school was the wrong choice and headed home. I didn't ask permission from anyone because I determined from there on out, *I was an adult.*

Dad wasn't home when I got there, which made me happy. I put my books on the table, grabbed a bath towel, and headed to the bathroom to take a shower. The water would soothe me, and I could think my next steps through. *How am I going to tell Dad that I hate him,* I thought. He ruined my life; he left me with no hopes to ever be normal.

Yeah, yeah, yeah, I understood medical breakthroughs were happening, and people like me were living longer and longer lives. It was also true that I could possibly have healthy children and marry in the future. But right then, my life was a lie, I continued to think.

The front door opened, and I heard bags rustling in the distance. Dad was home. Without thinking, I jumped out of the shower, wrapped a towel around my body, and shot to the kitchen.

"You lying bastard," I shouted. "How could you do this to me and Mama?" I said with hot tears blurring my vision.

Dad looked at me stunned. "Wait one minute, little girl. You will *not* talk to me in the tone, EVER!" he said back.

"You can't tell me how to talk to you. You're a liar, and a cheat—"

"Tasha, you better tone your voice down this minute or you *will* be sorry. Now go to your room and calm down, then we can speak."

"Go to my room? GO TO MY ROOM? Are you *serious?*" I started to shake. My hands felt numb, and my mouth began to twitch as I shivered. "Dad, how could you .

. . ."

"How could I what? What are you talking about, sweetheart?"

"How could you . . ." I fought to finish the sentence. "How could you sleep with your secretary and ruin our lives like this?"

Dad dropped the egg he was about to crack and it broke all over the floor. His body jerked as he tried to get his balance and put one hand on the stove and one on his chest. Not a word escaped from his lips. He just looked down at the floor.

"Who told you that?" he mumbled. I froze in fear. My dad's expressions were unfamiliar. He was a stranger to me in that instant.

"Is it true?" I asked unhappily.

Dad turned to look at me, but he couldn't. His eyes were fixed to the floor as he whispered, "Yes!"

In a fit of rage I knocked every pot from the stove, all the food from the table onto the floor, and ran to my room a hysterical mess. I couldn't take any more. I took hold of a bottle of sleeping pills from my purse and popped three. It was the next afternoon before I awoke.

Dad wasn't home. My head felt heavy, and my body ached. I went to the kitchen to get a sip of water when there was a knock on the door. It was Ty. At first I wanted to run and hide because my hair was a mess, and my clothes were crumply, but instead, I opened the door so he could see me in raw form.

"Dang, woman, you don't look any better. Are you okay?"

"No, I'm not okay and I don't want to talk about it, either. Come in," I responded. "I don't want to talk about anything if that's alright with you."

"No problem," he said solemnly. "We can just sit and watch TV. I came by because you haven't been answering your phone since you left school yesterday."

"Please excuse me for a minute." I left the living room to brush my teeth and wash my face as I heard Ty turn the TV on. When I returned, I sat as close to him as possible, he wrapped his arms around me, and we never spoke a word.

A few hours passed by, and still no sight of Daddy. I wanted to worry, but my heart wouldn't allow me to feel any pity for him after what he had done to me and my mother. Then, I heard voices in the yard that sounded a lot like Tris. It was him. He must have been home visiting Mia from college and just as I peeked through the front-room window to see if they were coming over, Mia and Tris rang the doorbell.

"Hey, y'all, come in. We're in the front room watching TV."

Triston seemed happy to have Ty there. "What's up, bro?" Tris said to Ty while they smacked each other's hands hard in a half-shake, half-hug greeting.

"I'm good, man, how's school?" Ty replied.

"Great, great . . ." They continued their male bonding when Mia signaled for me to come over. We went into my bedroom and shut the door.

"Girl," Mia said, "you look like shit. Is everything okay?"

I couldn't help but to break down; like normal Mia hugged me tightly, and we cried like babies in the middle of the floor. After I told her everything that happened, neither of us could move. All I remember after that was Mia saying, "You're a strong girl, you *will* get through this. *We* will get through this, sis." She was right. I had to get through it because I was getting downright sick of sorrow.

By the time we went back into the living room both of

us looked like crap. Mia told Tris that she was staying with me and asked him to drop Ty off when they were ready to go. Tris agreed. The guys left a couple hours later.

It was midnight, and Daddy still wasn't home. By then, both Mia and I began to worry. No matter what happened before, my father was still my savior, and I needed to know he that he was safe. We called around looking for him to no avail. Just as I was about to dial the emergency number, Dad's keys were jingling in the door and we both shot up to open it. He stumbled in. You could smell alcohol oozing from his pores as Mia and I helped him to bed, relieved he made it home safely.

"Mia," I said, "I'm in a lot of pain. I need to go to sleep. Are you cool on the couch?"

"I'll be right here, sis. If you need anything just call."

Before getting in bed I checked my phone. Ty left a message, and so did Mom. I checked Ty's and saved Mom's for the morning. He wanted to tell me that no matter what was going on, he was there for me and would never leave my side. I believed him.

The next morning Mia was in the kitchen fixing breakfast for us before she headed out to school. She made enough for her mom, too. After hearing all the problems my family was having, I guess she appreciated having a mother even more. I didn't want to stay home with Daddy alone so I got ready, too. I had to get out of the house. When Mia noticed I was dressed, she understood and said, "Come on, sis, let's roll."

I didn't bother to kiss Dad's forehead before leaving. "Tasha," I heard him call from his room, "are you leaving for school without saying good-bye?"

"Bye, Dad," I yelled from the hall, then hurried out and shut the door.

16 WHAT THE HELL?

Trying to figure out where I belonged after that day was tough. I lost the yearning to speak with Dr. Green, didn't want anything to do with Mom or Dad, and really cared less that Tris went away to school and Mia might follow. Some people would call what I was experiencing hopelessness. School became a ritual, and I just moved along like an ant following the colony. Two weeks later, I finally called Mom back and her apologies were plentiful. All I could do was hear her out because I suddenly had forgotten how to listen.

Mom expressed she never wanted me to find out the truth, especially not the way that I did, because that was the only promise she made to Dad—never to tell. I agreed with Dad, I never needed to know which parent did what, but it was too late for all that then. Mom and I didn't speak, and Dad and I hadn't said too much to each other either. That was the most pitiful I'd ever seen Dad, even with the illness.

When Mia stepped to me in the hall one day with the "I'm sorry look" on her face, I already knew what the deal was. I said it before she opened her mouth: "So you're going away to school with Tris, huh?"

Mia looked pathetically in my eyes. "I won't lie to you, Tasha, ever," she said. "Yep, I'm going away to school, and I'm pregnant."

I couldn't believe what I was hearing. We talked about right and wrong so much I just knew they had things all under control.

"You're *what?*"

"I found out yesterday. That's why I'm leaving."

"It's cool."

"It isn't cool. You know you don't have to hide your feelings with me girl."

"Naw, really, It's Okay . . .

"Let it out."

"Let what out?"

"Your feelings . . . happy, sad, whatever . . ."

Mia continued to tell me what I should and should not do, and how I should and shouldn't feel, when the truth was, I was *numb*. I felt enough hurt in my short life time to spread across a football field. As she went on with her premature motherly tangent, I lost focus.

"Tasha," Mia shouted, "did you hear *anything* I just said?" I shook my head *NO*, for I was tired of lying, too.

"I want you to be the baby's godmother."

I guess I should have been happy, but it was all too much for me at the moment. I hugged Mia, told her I loved her, and went looking for Ty. He was all I had left.

Ty was in class, so I went on to class too.

§

There was an announcement over the school's intercom that struck me hard. "Instead of a cancer walk this year, we will be participating in an HIV walk. Anyone who's interested, please come to the front office during lunch or study hall to sign up."

I couldn't believe what I had heard. My first thought was to ask Mia, but since the pregnancy, I didn't know if she'd be up to it so I asked Ty instead. He wasn't thrilled at first, but said "what the heck." His chemistry teacher offered extra credit to anyone who participated, so it was a win-win for him. I wanted to tell Daddy, too, but my pride wouldn't let me. We hadn't said two words to each other since he revealed the truth to me, and I began to wonder if I'd ever get over it and started hating Mom even more than before. I don't know why, but I did. For some reason I felt she told me her secret to clear her own conscious, not to help my life, and that angered me day and night. Anyhow, I figured doing the walk would put me in the presence of like-minded folk, who were walking for a cause that could help my family. I needed to be in a positive space.

When the bell rang, I searched for Mia to ask her anyway; heck, what could it hurt? To my surprise, before I could speak, "Did you hear the announcement?" Mia was more excited than I. "So will we do it?" she asked.

"Hell, yeah, I want to do it."

It was set. Mia, Tris, and Ty would be joining me on my private crusade to save the world on our first ever fundraising event. The guys had no idea why we were so eager, but that didn't matter. By the end of the day I was pooped, and although I dreaded going home, I didn't want to be anywhere else but in my own bed. Daddy was gone when I got there, surprisingly. I took a quick shower and was knocked out cold in a matter of minutes. I slept so sound, I didn't hear Daddy come in or go to his room, but he did and was taking a nap when I awakened. My stomach ached with hunger so I pranced to the kitchen to grab some grub. There was a sales paper on the table turned to the page of hunting gear; was daddy planning a hunting trip, I wondered. He brought back a Subway sandwich and left it on the stove for me. It was right on time.

Marching to the living room with my plate balanced in front of my chest, I turned on the TV and chilled. Just as I wrapped my mouth around the last sloppy piece, the phone rang and it was my annoying mother.

"HELLO," I shouted through the receiver, licking my fingers at the same time.

"Hey, honey, I just wanted to check on you and your father. How is everything over there?"

"Okay," I said quickly.

"Can I stop by later?"

"Why?"

"Tasha, because I need to see you guys and apologize in person," my mother declared.

I was not in the mood to keep reliving that nightmare and agreed just so she had no other excuses to ever bring it up again. I went to Dad's room to alert him of her visit. He wasn't happy at all but got up to put clothes on anyway.

Dad didn't put up a fuss and didn't ask me how I felt about it; he simply worked his way around his room slowly grabbing different items from his closet. In the end, he settled for his pajamas and a robe and said, "What's the use in getting dressed anyway?"

"Wow," I thought, dad was still trying to impress mom up until that very moment. I felt so sorry for him.

Mom was there in less than two hours. It was all done in my eyes, but as usual, she had to have it her way. When she got out of the car, I unlocked the door so she wouldn't have to knock. Although I hadn't spoken to Dad much either, I sat on the couch where he was so I didn't have to sit next to her when my phone started ringing in the other room. It was a quick skip to the purse.

"Hey, Mia," I said.

"Girl, is that your mom's car?" she asked.

"Yep, she's here and I don't know why," I said sarcastically.

"Is everything okay over there?"

"She wants to apologize in person, I'll call you back with details when she leaves."

"Alright, girl, bye."

"Bye." I walked as slowly as possible back to the living room.

Mom didn't waste any time taking the floor, *again.* "I needed to tell you both how terribly sorry I am for breaking a promise that has torn us completely apart." Dad and I both looked on as she reached in her purse for a tissue, already tearing up. "I don't know what came over me that day at the doctor's office, and I will always regret what I did and how I went about it. Do you guys understand?" she questioned.

I didn't answer. I had no answer to give her, but I was shocked when Daddy shot right in and asked, "Are you asking us for forgiveness, Cali?" His question was asked in such a way that Mom hesitated to answer. She knew to ask Dad for forgiveness after all the times he'd asked to be forgiven was like opening a spoiled meat package to eat. She looked at me, and then glanced over at him with her eyes slowly lowering to the floor.

"John, please, let's not fight . . ." She paused in the middle of her sentence to blow her nose. "I was wrong for what I did to Tasha, but I wasn't wrong for not forgiving you."

"M-O-M," I shouted, "are you serious?"

"What do you mean am I serious? Yes, I'm serious."

She and I went back and forth about what's wrong-is-wrong and right-is-right that we never noticed Dad stand up and go into his bedroom. He was too weak to fight and didn't care to hear us argue to and fro. To openly hear mother declare, that after all was said and done, she still refused to forgive him was probably his final breaking point. All the extras were just too much for him. "Mom, are you done talking? If so; may I please be excused?" She sat there shaking her head in disbelief.

She stood up, asked for a hug, I obliged and told her, "I don't know where this leaves us, but all I ever wanted was to be normal and to belong to a normal family. Drive safe."

She hugged me back and said, "Tasha, I love you, and we are normal, and you do belong to a normal family. I'll call you later."

That time was different though. I didn't cry. There was an unrecognizable strength I held. That was it. My mind was made up. I wasn't going to let the disease destroy the life I had left, and although it was going to be difficult to forgive my parents, I was determined to do it. I went into Dad's room and sat at the foot of his bed like he normally did to me.

"Dad, I don't know why Mom never forgave you, and I don't know if I'll ever be able to forgive you, but I'm going to try." He didn't say a word. I touched his ankle gently, holding my hand there for a moment before leaving the room. As I exited, I whispered, "And I want to go live with Mom."

I knew living with my Mother wasn't going to work because we never saw eye-to-eye. However, if we were under the same roof, I could try regularly to help her see the benefits of forgiving Dad. One reason I wanted to do it was because I needed her to so I could move forward, the other was so we could start repairing our broken family. It was my vow that our statuses would no longer control us.

That night I sat at the kitchen table reading some mail, and I ran across a letter from Dad's specialists. Basically, it said his treatments were not rendering the results they were hoping for, and that they wanted him to participate in a study for a trial drug being tested.

No wonder Dad didn't have any energy to fight with Mom, I thought. I instantly felt bad but kept hoping for the best for him.

§

Saturday came quickly. Everyone met up at Tris's house since he was in town from school. We all wore red tees and red and white gym shoes. Ty slipped his fingers into mine on the couch and pulled me up. As soon as we stepped in the hall, Ty pulled me close, put his hands behind both sides of my head, and kissed me passionately. We were still kissing when Mia and Tris walked out and caught us in the act. Tris said, "Y'all can go back in the spot for a while. Moms' is gone."

"Shut up, boy. Let's go y'all," Mia said kind of annoyed at Triston's lack of maturity.

It was hot that day, and there were lots of people there. Blotches of red was scattered all about the park. The walk began, and we were off. Tris and Mia hung in there with us for a while, but I knew with the heat and the baby in her belly she would fall behind—and they did.

"Tasha," Ty said, "do you think all these people are infected? He asked with his face frowned up.

"Nope, why?"

"Just curious."

I couldn't help but wonder why he thought that but

didn't care to talk about it anymore. Instead, I walked ahead of him picking up informational pamphlets along the way, putting them in my backpack. Ty started people watching again and said, "It's a hell of a lot of gays out here."

"Why do you say that," I said annoyed.

"Look at those men over there holding hands, that's why."

Extremely irritated, I asked, "And what . . .? Do you have a problem with them?"

"Naw babe, as long as they stay away from me," he replied.

I was so frustrated I couldn't resist asking, "Who gave you the right to judge?"

He looked at me shamefully, "did I offend you?"

I went on a ten-minute tirade about stereotypes and stigmas and the like and by the time I rested my vocal cords he was apologizing. "Man, babe, you got upset," he said hugging me.

"None of it was directed toward you, boo." I knew he didn't mean to hurt my feelings. But I felt like *I* was *those* people he referred to.

We met up with Tris and Mia at the water station, Mia

was eating an apple with an innocent look on her face.

"Come on, guys, let's go have lunch. This was fun," I said.

17 LIVING WITH MOM

I wanted the move with Mom to be temporary so I didn't take many of my things. Each day I chipped away at her heart by pressing the issue of forgiving Dad. And one day, it just worked. She said, "Honey, I have forgiven him."

"You have?" I said to her, and she nodded yes.

Mom explained how she suffered many dark nights by holding onto the past. I asked her to tell me more about what was going on back then so I could understand what they were up against.

Mom told me Dad hated that she was never in the mood for intimacy during her pregnancy with me and he always complained how her attitude was a bit chilly toward him. She went on to say how their talks about affection turned into full-blown arguments. They would go days not speaking to one another. "The house typically became a war zone."

"Did you ever have a hunch that his secretary was interested in him?" I asked her.

"Kind of. She would do little extras like take his clothes to the cleaners or buy him gifts for his birthday."

"Really?"

"Uh-huh . . ."

"One day I wanted to surprise him with lunch and she lied to me."

"Really mom? About what?"

"She said your father left the office an hour before I got there on a business lunch and had yet to return, so I sat in the parking lot waiting for him to come back. When he never returned, I marched into his office furious and he was sitting at the desk on a conference call."

"What mom? What did you do?"

"I stormed to the reception area and gave that tramp a piece of mind. All she said was, "I'm sorry Mrs. Davis, I guess he snuck in without me noticing."

"That's a shame," I said.

"I found out later from your father that she never told him I was even there and that he never even left the office that day." Looking at Mom through a new lens, something erupted inside. I finally understood that my mother wasn't as cold as ice; she was human. We giggled a bit at the story but I knew the laughs wouldn't last long because the look on her face changed for the worse.

Finally the moment came I dreaded to hear. Mother said one night Dad didn't come home. He said he went out drinking with the guys and didn't want to risk a DUI. She believed him at first . . . until she found a hotel receipt weeks later in the back of his car.

"But we were working through it, became intimate once more, and were getting closer. I don't think your dad ever saw that woman again after that night because she resigned the day after they slept together."

"Insane," I mumbled.

"Two months passed and I had a doctor's appointment. It was a regular checkup, breast exam, Pap smear, and I was screened for STD's," mom said reaching for the tissue. She began to tear up once again. "I went home like normal, continued breast-feeding you and enjoyed my family. Your dad and I had fallen in love again. Funny how bad things can actually bring people closer. That is, until I got the call I would never forget: 'Mrs. Davis, we need you and Tasha to come to the clinic. We can't give you any information over the phone.'"

Mother paused, cleared her throat, "And when I got there it was revealed to me that I was HIV-positive, and they needed to test you since I breast-fed. That was the hardest day of my life. I don't think I can ever experience pain again like I felt that day. I looked at you wrapped in your little blanket and hope for the best as the nurse drew your blood." *Sniff, Sniff, Sniff* . . . my mother cried.

By the end of the story I simply said, "But it's over now, Mom. We're living. That's all we can ask for." I didn't shed a tear. It was time to fight for my life, and I needed her to be strong so we could be strong for Daddy. He was the one not doing so well, and I wanted that to change.

I called Dad's phone, but he didn't pick up. "Mom," I asked, "can we go back and talk to Daddy? I should have never left him."

"How about I go alone? You stay here. Maybe he has some things he wants to share with me without you there."

I agreed, and Mom left. I called Ty to pass some time because I needed to hear his jokes. He was always a ball of fun, at any given moment.

"So how long is your mother gone for?" Ty questioned.

"I don't know. Why?" I answered.

"Because I'm on my way to see you."

"Really?"

"Yep," he said. I told him okay, and he came.

It wasn't even the middle of the movie before Ty had my one breast in his mouth while squeezing the other one. I could have gotten used to simply making out since I had yet to disclose my secret to him, but I could tell he wanted more.

"Come on, Tasha," he grunted.

"No, my mother could come home any second." I knew Mom must have stopped off somewhere because she was gone for a few hours, but that excuse was good enough to use to stall him.

That was the first time I saw Ty aggravated. He didn't understand why I was holding out for so long. He stopped right in the middle of a kiss and asked, "Do you want me to see other girls or something? I ain't gon' wait forever, Tasha."

I knew he was serious and had been the perfect boyfriend to me for all I knew and heard, and I didn't want to lose him.

My phone started ringing in my bag. I told Ty to let me grab it, but instead, he held me down, rubbing and touching my body. The phone rang again and again, so I push him off me as I jumped up, "I gotta answer it," I said. I was afraid it might be serious since whoever it was called back-to-back several times. It was my mom. There was seven missed calls total. I tried calling back, but she didn't answer. I called her two more times, still no answer. I got worried and called Mia.

"Hey, Tasha," she said, "what's up?"

"Favor. Do you see my mom's car out front?"

I could hear clanking as Mia put the phone down to go look. "Yep, it's out there. What's going on?"

"I don't know. She just called a few times, and now she isn't picking up. Can you walk over there and check on things?"

"Sure, you want me to call you back—"

I cut her off midsentence. "No, I want to stay on the line."

"O-k-a-y . . ."

I could hear Mia walking to my house, and then I heard faint sounds of commotion.

"Tasha, I think I hear crying."

I froze and didn't know what to say while Ty kept asking me what was going on. "I don't know yet, babe," I said to him.

As Mia got closer to the house I could hear my mother shouting, "Put it down, John, please don't do this."

I began crying and screaming, "Mia, hurry!"

I heard Mia twisting frantically on the door handle. It was locked, but she had a key to our house for as long as I could remember. She knocked hard before using it to open the door.

"What's going on over there?" Ty kept asking.

"I DON'T FUCKING KNOW," I said shouting at him at the top of my lungs.

He got up and stood as close to me as possible while rubbing my back. "I'm sorry, babe," he whispered.

Boom! "What was that?" I said to Mia. She didn't answer. "WHAT WAS THAT?" I shouted, still no answer.

There was a bunch of rumbling and crackling on the phone then complete chaos reigned in the house. All I could hear was Mia and Mother crying and shouting for help.

"John," I heard my mother say, "I forgive you. Please don't do this."

At the same time Mia was pleading, "Please, Dad, don't do it. Don't do it, Mr. Davis." It was hard to make out everything but I know I never heard my father's voice at all. Immediately afterward, I heard a quick POP, a loud thud, then a piercing scream from Mom. The phone disconnected.

I fainted.

When I came to, Ty was holding me on the floor with a cool towel pressed firmly to my forehead. After a couple of blinks Ty whispered, "The ambulance is on its way." I could do nothing but lie there and sob. I had no desire to call Mia back and confirm what I thought just happened. I didn't want to see the disturbed, guilty look on Mother's face. I didn't want to hear one person tell me it was going to be okay. All I wanted to do was see my father's face, hear his voice, but that was only a dream.

When the ambulance pulled up, I met them outside. I didn't want them in my mother's house. I didn't want to go to the hospital either. I just wanted to run away.

The next twenty hours or so were some of the most confusing times of my life because I really didn't understand what had happened. Or why even. There were lots of visitors in and out of my hospital room, but I don't remember saying anything to any of them. Only one person stood out, Ty's mother. I remember her and Ty walking into the room with flowers and a card, and she told me if there was anything she could do, to please call her. "Ty and I will make sure you have anything that you need," she said. But I will never forget the look on her face. She looked down at me with the most pitiful eyes I'd ever seen.

My mother gave me free reign on all funeral decisions. I knew my dad the best. He had few friends, came from a very small family, and his only brother preceded him in death five years prior. I wanted the entire family to wear baby blue tops, while I chose dad's favorite dark blue suit as a contrast. I had to tell Mother by phone where the suit actually was because she did not allow me back into the house until all the remodeling had been done in the area where it all happened. It made sense. I didn't need to see it, nor would I ever have wanted to see it. I wanted to remember my dad's smooth, delightful demeanor just as I'd always known. His actions would not change that.

When I was released from the hospital a day and a half

later, I went to Mother's. The house was packed which suffocated me. I walked past at least twenty people without even speaking or greeting a single soul. Mia followed me into my room, and Chida followed her. My jeans were down to my ankles when they walked in. I didn't care and changed into a set of pajamas left on my bed and slowly, crawled under the covers with my back to them. Neither of the girls said a word. Chida sat in the chair next to my bed and Mia plopped directly behind me placing her hand gently on the small of my back. I heard sniffles and nose blowing, but didn't want to turn around and look to see who it was.

Many questions crept in my head about that night I wanted to ask Mia, but didn't have the energy to listen to it, and damn sure didn't want to cry. So I drifted off instead. When I woke up, Mia was balled up in a corner of my bed sleeping soundly, and Chida was gone. Reaching for my phone on the floor beside me, I woke Mia up. I had four missed calls, three from Ty, and the other, Dr. Green.

"How do you feel?" I asked Mia.

"Okay, but what about you?" she responded.

"Alright, I guess. My chest has been bothering me."

"Did you tell that to the doctor?"

"Yep." That was all I was ready to say at the moment. There didn't seem to be a need for constant chatter.

I stood up to grab the door handle and Mia asked, "Tasha, are you okay? You seem—"

Stopping her immediately, "I'm fine," I said, and walked out the door. The house cleared out a bit, but the remaining eyes left gazed at me as I entered the living room.

"Hey, y'all," I said lowly and kept walking, praying no one responded with an open-ended question.

"Tasha, I'm in the kitchen," mom shouted.

She and my aunt were sitting at the table looking at pictures for the obituary and asked if I had a favorite. Nodding my head up and down, I reached on the top of the refrigerator for my little keepsake box and gave them a picture I took of Daddy one day at the park. When they saw it, Mom immediately teared up. Wiping her eyes with a tissue she said, "I remember this day."

"How, Mom? You weren't with us," I stated.

"I was, you just didn't know it." I looked at her confused.

"I was missing you and called your dad to ask if I could come by."

181

"Really?" I asked.

"Yep. He said you guys were at the park so I drove there."

"I never saw you." I immediately thought this was just another one of her stories, but she kept going. When she mentioned what I had on that day, I knew she was there.

"I never got up the nerve to come inside the playground, so I sat and watched y'all from the car."

"Humph, I never knew that, Mom."

"Neither did your dad," she said, and then asked to be excused for a moment. I knew she was going somewhere to cry in private. My mother didn't like people to view her as weak. I guess that's where I got it from.

In the sink was a plate I made for Dad in the fourth grade with my handprints stained on it. I wondered why Mom pulled it out as I poured a glass of water. As soon as I put the glass to my mouth my aunt asked if I was okay. I nodded my head slowly, never taking the glass from my lips, hoping it would stop her from questioning me. Mia came into the kitchen looking for something to eat. Her belly was getting bigger, and I felt bad everything was happening to her while she was pregnant with my godchild.

"Mia, you were there when it happened, weren't you?" my aunt blurted out.

"Aunt Faye, I don't want to hear about that," I said angrily. "Why do you want to know anyway? H-U-H?"

"Tasha, don't speak to me in that tone, please."

"What tone?"

Before the argument could go any further Mia said, "Yes, I was there, but I don't want to talk about it now."

Apparently my nosey aunt got upset because she stormed out of the kitchen. I overheard her tell one of my mother's employees that she would talk to her later; she was leaving. So I yelled into the living room, "Bye, Aunt Faye."

Any other time Mia and I would have erupted in laughter afterwards, but that wasn't one of those times. We did look at each other and grinned, however. It was kind of funny. I thought, *the nerve of some people.*

I still didn't have an appetite, but I sat in the kitchen while Mia scoffed down some Mostacholli and BBQ'd baked beans while other family and friends chatted in the living area.

"Chida told me to tell you she would be back tomorrow if it was alright with you," Mia remembered in between scoops of beans.

"That's cool," I said. "Will Tris make it to the

funeral?"

"Yep . . .talked to him this morning."

"Cool."

"Tasha . . ." There was a pause so Mia was obviously trying to make sure she had my undivided attention.

"Huh?" I replied.

"If you ever want to talk about it, I'm always here and ready to do it, okay?"

"I know," I replied, "and there's lot I want to ask, but I'd rather not think about it right now."

"Understood," Mia said.

But I thought of one question I needed to know right then and there. "Did Dad mention me? When . . . you know . . . that day he . . ."

Mia teared up, "Yeah, he did. He looked directly at me and said, 'Mia, tell Tasha I'm sorry.'"

In that instant, once again, the sobbing duo was drenched in tears. Mia got up from her seat, took me by the hand, and we scurried to the bathroom. I think we were in there for over an hour, crying, hugging, cleaning our faces, then we cried, hugged, and cleaned some more. Mother knocked on the door hysterically asking, "Are you girls all right in there?"

"Yes," we replied in our old-fashioned unison tone.

At the end of the day, my dad was gone and all I could do was ask, why me?

§

There was nothing exciting or memorable about the funeral. I can't even tell you who was there and who wasn't. It was all a blur. I know Mother sat on my left side and Mia on my right. Ty and his mother sat in the row behind us, with Tris, Dr. Green, Dr. Beech, Chida, and Tachell. The church was packed, but I can't name another soul present. I rejected the opportunity to speak when the obituary was made out because I didn't think I would be able to do it. But something compelled me to get up when they asked for two-minute remarks from the public. When I rose from my seat, I felt faint and fear ran through me like an infection. But someone started clapping and before you knew it, most people in the church were standing to their feet applauding me, and I was somehow encouraged.

"Many of you in this church today don't have a father or can't remember the last time you and your father sat at a

dinner table together. Many of you lost contact with your fathers along the way, for whatever reason. But I got to know my father up close and personal, and there is nothing I wouldn't do to eat across the table with him again." I held my head back to try and keep the tears from falling.

"It's okay, Tasha," someone yelled from the back of the church. *"Gone, Girl."*

I continued. *"My father combed my hair, and I still remember kids teasing me about my crooked parts. But that was one of the things that made us special. He was a one-of-a-kind dad, and I don't want anyone in the room today leaving here thinking he was selfish for his actions. I don't want anyone in this room today to leave here gossiping about him being weak. My father was great, he was magnificent, and he was, I mean is, My Hero!"*

I stepped down from the podium, and the applause and praise were so loud the preacher started shouting. Mother was crying, her chest heaved up and down. Mia met me in the aisle and hugged me as we maneuvered back to our seats. I know she wanted to cry, but she held on for me since I hadn't shed a tear. I had a breakthrough at Dad's funeral. I was on a crusade to save lives. I wanted to leave a legacy like my father left with me. His death would not go in vain.

Ty sat with me during the entire repast. I cried on his shoulders, we danced, we laughed, and enjoyed the moment. Mom and Ms. Johnson talked quite a bit as well. Tris and Mia ate like pigs. I giggled every time I saw them at the food table. I guess they were both eating for two. Chida even apologized for us not being as close as we were in grammar school and said things would change. Dr. Green stopped by the dance floor on her way out of the repast and asked me if I wanted to resume our meetings, alone. I agreed, "see you Friday." All I heard was Ty saying, "Come on, Tasha, let me see your footwork." We danced and partied the night away.

Mother got me a home schoolteacher for a few weeks so I wouldn't fall behind in my studies, but I was ready to go home. It felt good to connect with Mom and everything, but her house simply didn't comfort me.

Of all people my mother could ask to live with me, I overheard her on the phone with Aunt Faye asking her to do it. Without delay, I fanned my hand in the air trying to get her attention, then waved my right hand across my neck in a slicing motion. There was no way I would agree to being roommates with nosey Aunt Faye. Mom noticed my behavior, "Faye look, let me call you back. Tasha, what was that all about? You know you can't stay in that house alone."

"I know Mom, but not her."

"Then who?"

"I don't know, but not her," I said firmly. "Why can't Mia do it until she leaves for college in August?"

"I'm not sure that's a good idea. She's not that much older than you."

"Yeah, but her mom is right next door, and I can help her with the baby."

"Tasha, I don't even know if that's legal. How old is she?"

"Eighteen. She turned eighteen in November."

A protective, concerned look grew on her face. I basically continued to give reasons why I felt Mia would be the best fit for me and how I knew Mrs. Bolden would be okay with it all. What I didn't want mom to do was think about it too hard. That never went well.

"Okay," she finally said.

"Okay, what?"

"Mia can stay there until she goes to school. But if I

hear anything, and I do mean *anything* out of order, we are selling the condo, and you're moving back here with me in Roselle."

I jumped up and embraced Mom with all my might. "Thank you, thank you," I said running to my room to grab my cell phone and tell Mia the news.

18 PUTTING HIGH SCHOOL BEHIND THEM

Clouds covered the sky, and my instincts told me we would be washed out. However, by noon, the rain had fallen, sky cleared up, and it was a beautiful day. Mom rented two rooms of the banquet hall, one for the shower, the other for the party.

There were pink carriages and pacifiers hanging from the ceiling, and two stork ice sculptures that decorated neighboring tables. Melted water from the storks drained into a crystal tub that had miniature plastic, pink and green storks floating around in them. It was absolutely beautiful.

In the room intended for the graduation party, the DJ booth was covered with caps and gowns. Mom had a disco ball draped from the ceiling in the middle of the room and when lit, it projected colorful diplomas all across the area in fluorescent lights. To this day, I still don't know where my mother found it.

Since it was a surprise, Tris told Mia they were going

to visit family members for a trunk party in her honor. Mia had no idea he was lying. I called Tris to make sure the plan was running smoothly.

"Yep," he said. "I got this. Don't worry yourself, Ty's lover girl. Daddy Tris got it all under control." He was always joking and playful-like.

When I hung up the phone I was thrilled, bubbling with excitement. Ty arrived early just as we planned; I had a surprise for him, too. There was a little dark room I found in the banquet area and when he got there I took him in so we could have a make-out session like never before, since I wasn't eager in any way to have sex yet. I had to be creative when thinking of ways to keep my man happy.

Pushing my back forcibly against the wall and holding my chin up as we kissed passionately, he said, "Tasha, baby" (*kiss, kiss . . .*), "why can't we go all the way?" (*kiss, kiss . . .*)

"We will."

"When?"

"H-u-h?"

"When, baby? I need you."

I thought about all the things I needed to figure out before we could make that move. Yet, I never shared my thoughts with Ty so I understood his growing impatience. "Soon enough, but let's just enjoy this for now!" I said convincingly as I gently bit his bottom lip.

"I'm ready when you are . . ." he said, looking breathlessly into my eyes.

He would not trap me into committing to dates so I took hold of his hand and led the way. "We gotta go before everyone starts looking for us."

He walked close behind me, hands wrapped around my waist. "We gotta get in place. She should be coming in soon."

The hall was pretty long with crystal chandeliers shining brightly overhead. There were so many people there that brought gifts; boxes were lined halfway across the largest wall of the room. It would take days to sift through all of that stuff.

"Surprise!" roared throughout the space, and the lights flickered when we saw a body coming through the door. It was Triston.

"Tasha," he called out.

"I'm over here," I said confused. "Where's Mia?"

Tris jogged over to me. "She won't get out of the car," he whispered in my ear.

"Why not?"

"We argued on the way. Come with me. She'll listen to you."

Just as I was about to go with Tris to the car and ruin the whole thing, "Surprise!" blasted out in the room once more.

As she realized what was going on, I ran over to her. "Awww, don't cry. I love you, sis."

She gave me one of the longest hugs ever. My shoulder was damp when she finally let go. I said happily, "Go mingle."

Mia disappeared into the crowd of people who waited patiently for their turn to call her *crybaby*. We got the shower started, but poor Mia had no idea how long of a night she was up against.

Her aunt passed out rules and toys for the games we played while pencils and scramble words sheets covered the tables. One group of older women wrapped their teammates in toilet paper trying to win the prize for best tissue diaper. While another group watched and giggled. It was magnificent. After everyone had eaten and all the games were done, it was time for Mia to open her gifts. That was the longest gift opening session I'd ever seen. It took at least an hour and a half to get to them all.

The older bunch crept out of the hall during the gift presentation looking pooped. I just knew Mia would find it weird that the old folks were walking out but younger ones filed in, arriving in groups at a time. Mia would say, "Late . . . all the cake is gone."

Some laughed at her, "It's cool as long as we didn't miss everything," because they knew their party hadn't started yet.

"I am so tired," Mia said to me. "I just want to crawl in Dad's bed and go to sleep." My insides were tickled.

After the last person who wasn't staying for the graduation party left the shower, I said, "Ah, let's go home, sis."

Mia followed me out of one room and into the next. It was pitch-black in there. I said the cue line, "Wait Mia, let me find the light switch. I left my bag in here."

At exactly the right moment, the lights came on and "Surprise!" rang out so loud my ears popped. Mia scanned the room in total disbelief. You would have thought our entire high school was there. The music sounded on while Mia stood in the middle of the floor crying like a baby just as Chida and a few other friends were headed her way.

They took Mia by the hand, escorting her out of the room. When they eventually came back from the bathroom, she partied hard with her belly popping up and down to the beat of the music, refusing to be outdone by her flat-stomach classmates.

My mother kept out of view, but I kept glancing her way, giving her the thumbs-up. She did a magnificent job and her ideas were brought to life. Deep inside, I kind of felt she loved Mia more than me, but it didn't matter, I loved Mia, too! My best friend in the world was having the time of her life, and it gave me an allover tingling sensation.

Mom and I made parting bags for everyone. Inside were all types of little graduation keepsakes: bookmarks, pendants, and chocolates. We even had special red ribbons and miniature STD packets in there, too. For the first time in my life, I didn't fear if the guests would question why certain materials were tucked away in the bag. It was for a good cause, as far as I was concerned. It was elevating.

As the stragglers filed out of the hall, Mia and Tris went over to my mother and embraced in a three-way hug. Tris couldn't believe the amount of things the baby had gotten. He had nothing to stress over but the physical birth.

"Starting off alone in a new state won't be so bad afterall. Will it, babe?" he asked Mia.

She was so overwhelmed she choked on her words, "I g-u-e-s-s not." It took all three cars getting that stuff back to my house. Mother said her good-byes to us, and we went back to my place.

Tris glanced over at Ty with a fatherly look. "Man, what time is your mom expecting you home?"

"Don't know. I'll call from Tasha's." Ty looked at Mia, and Mia looked at me with a look I recognized. In other words, there would not be any spending the night for Ty or Tris.

"You guys can come over for a bit, but then you gotta go," she said sharply to them. "It's late."

"We know, Mama Mia," Tris sprang out jokingly. "We know."

And with a light kiss to the cheek Mia replied, "Good."

After the guys carried everything inside Ty said, "Tasha, I'm done for the night. I'm beat."

"Me, too. Thanks for coming. Thanks for all your help pulling it off."

"No problem. Anything for you and Mia. Anything." We gave each other a small peck on the lips, and he left.

Tris stayed awhile longer since Mia was still so very emotional. I saw Triston's eyelids sagging as he stood up, "OK, boo, I'm out." Mia walked Tris to the door and turned to me, "I'm gone to bed, Tasha. I can't cry another tear or hold my eyelids open any longer."

"Okay," was all I remember saying.

I woke up the next morning on the couch dressed in yesterday's clothes. As I stood up, stretching my arms towards the ceiling, I could see Dad's room door open and Mia in his bed sleeping like a chubby baby. The room was filled with baby stuff. Toys, blankets, and cards of well wishes were scattered all over the floor, Mia had to have opened them all before falling asleep.

I sat on the floor, picking up one card at a time, reading what people had written. "Congrats on your bundle of joy, Love Aunt Chynine." There was one card that was really cute and appeared to be homemade. As I reached over to my far left to pick it up, I noticed a shiny box jammed between the frame of the bed and the box spring. It was not my intention to wake Mia, so I crawled quietly on all fours to take a closer look. Moving the box back and forth it loosened, then in one quick yank it was out.

The first thing to catch my attention was a set of

wedding rings planted nicely inside. Never had I seen Mother or Father wear rings which is why I always assumed there were none. They were beautiful. Engraved inside, "Mr. and Mrs. Davis," was set in an Old English font. Holding both rings in my palms, I drew my closed hands close to my chest and held them there for a moment. As I slowly opened them, I took Mother's ring into my right hand and put it on my left ring finger, and then I held it up to my face to admire its beauty and how perfectly it fit. A tear dripped from my eye, rolled down my cheek, and plopped right on the shiny silver box. It was mine. I would keep it forever.

Eager to see what else was inside I picked the box up from the floor and noticed it, too, was engraved "Mr. & Mrs. Davis." It was disheartening to hold their marriage and divorce certificates in my hand.

Mia rolled over. I thought I had awakened her, but she was readjusting her position. A few old pictures of Mom when she was younger were caught in between the certificates and some other folded papers. *Wow,* I thought, *we look just alike.* I took my time admiring each photo, placing one behind the other. Inside the box were baby pictures of me and a folded envelope at the very bottom.

My mind raced. Since the day he died, I always wondered about a letter, some type of explanation, of why Dad chose to leave so suddenly. Honestly, I didn't hate my dad for ending what he considered a miserable life. I hated how he didn't say good-bye. I hated wondering if he even thought about how I would feel. I hated that he felt he had to choose between life and death, but I could never, ever, hate the man that gave me so much. How he went about it haunted me but something in my conscious said I found the missing link. I was about to get the closure I needed.

The envelope fell on the floor twice from my trembling hands and "Dear Tasha" sprang out at me like floodgates opening. After taking a deep breath I read the letter softly. *Dear Tasha,*

By the time you get this letter I will be gone. You will hear all sorts of stories about who I am, what I was, and why I did what I did. But, sweetheart, no one on this huge round earth knows me better than you. I bet you're thinking, "Daddy chose death over me." I can just see your face as I write this letter saying, "Daddy, you can beat this thing." I tried, Tasha, but it was too late. I fought the disease for as long as I could and lost my will to fight any longer. The stomachaches, night sweats, nightmares, and

199

physical weakness all turned out to be too much for me to handle. But, baby girl, my sweet, sweet, baby girl, it had nothing to do with you or your mother. I need you to do me a favor. With me gone, all you have left that knows your struggle is your mother. Please try to love her freely and unconditionally. She means well.

Tasha, I really wish I could have moved past the embarrassment I endured when Sheila gave me this disease. I wish I could have gotten past it and did what I had to do to stay healthy. But I couldn't—I just couldn't. There was always this overwhelming fear that someone would see me going to a treatment center. A fear someone would find out and spread the word to my staff. I thought I had been handed an unofficial death sentence. Then the thought of me spreading this thing to the two most important women in my life was unbearable. To me, my life ended the day the two of you were diagnosed. Wipe your eyes, Princess, because I know you're crying now.

He was right; tears were streaming at a constant rate.

After I saw how bright you were on your graduation day, I found some fight left deep inside. I realized I wanted to live and be a part of all your milestones to come. I don't know if you ever knew this or not, but my body rejected or resisted every treatment offered to me. I waited too late to be helped. Everything I did from then on was only to ease my pain.

I instantly thought back to the letter I saw on the table about test drugs. My heart was then being tugged in every direction.

It was another stubborn decision of mine to not say anything. I felt it was best not to put any more burden on you or your mom. In the end, I just couldn't bear the pain anymore; my body and mind were tired. I know that it's wrong, and I pray one day you will not only forgive me, but also move on with your life. Live the happiest life you possibly can and never, ever, feel sorry for yourself or for me. Truth is, and you know I never told you anything but the truth, I was going to die soon anyway. None of the treatments they tried worked. I waited too late and had been issued a prognosis. Tasha, honey, don't let life beat you like it did me. Never stop your treatment and never lose sight of your purpose. We all have one. I love you, Tasha. Bye, sweetheart.

Love, Dad

19 BEST FRIEND BLUES

Mia's pregnancy flew by, and so did my junior year. By then, she was round and plump, ready to burst. The time went so fast there were moments I don't even remember anymore. After school one afternoon, Mia plopped her body into the recliner chair in the living room but she had to lean backward first in order to sit. It was a sight to see on such a slim frame. Her breathing was heavier by the time her bottom rested in the chair. In between deep breathes, she said, "I know this is a lot to ask, but would you take me to D.C. to look for an apartment?" I rolled my eyes in her direction, "Umm . . . yeah, I'm down for a road trip."

Watching Mia prepare to move on with her life was hard for me, but a trip sounded exciting.

"I still hate you have to go."

"I know, sweet thang," Mia giggled, "but I'm always here, no matter how far, girl." She shifted her entire body around. It took a second for her huge belly to make the full turn.

"So . . . I decided to just do community college," Mia said doubtfully. I asked why with a scrunched forehead.

"Because," she sighed, "I don't know anything about being a mother. Its best I take it slow ya' know. Give myself time to adjust." That was never Mia's plan. She always wanted to go straight from high school to a university so I knew she was disappointed.

"True . . . So what did Tris say? He knows this isn't what you want."

Mia's already strained smiled drooped further. "Um, he . . ."

"He what?"

Mia was holding back. There was more to tell, but the words just weren't there.

"I think he's seeing another girl," she blurted out.

"Whoa . . . Wait, wait. What?" I said with bucked eyes. That was a total shock and definitely unexpected. What I didn't understand was, if that was the case, why move all the way to D.C. if he didn't want to be with her anymore. "Maybe that's all in your mind, Mia. Tris has always been such a good guy. Sarcastic but good."

"Good guys make mistakes too, Tasha." The empty

look in her eyes signaled the end of that conversation.

We packed quietly preparing to hit the road. My senior year gift from Mom was a shiny black Ford Explorer so there was plenty of room for me and Mia's big belly. We jammed all types of treats in a small cooler and put it on the floor in the back.

"Pass me a pack of cookies, Mia." She smirked, got two packs of cookies, one for me and one for her and then we hit the road.

"You never told me how you came up with the rest of the money for the apartment."

With squinted eyes and a confused expression she responded, "I didn't?"

"Naw, girl, you didn't."

"Come to find out my Mom had a college fund for me she'd been saving since I was a baby."

"Word?"

"Yep—it was for my future, but since the baby became a part of my future first, she gave it to me."

"Dang. That's what's up then."

Ring, Ring.

It was my mother. I forgot to tell her that we we're leaving like she asked me to, "We're on the road, Mom, and I'm driving. Call you back later." I didn't even wait to hear her respond before ending the call.

It was both of our first time in D.C.. Tris never wanted Mia traveling back and forth being pregnant and all, so he would take the trip to Chicago to see her instead.

Being on the open road and seeing new sights was awesome. We both knew there were some pretty rough areas in D.C., but Mia was determined to live as close to Howard's campus as possible. However, a few places she considered were a bit out of her price range but I instantly thought of mom; someone I knew would help their ends meet, especially if it meant the baby got to live in a safe environment. I was right.

"This is the one," Mia shouted, covering her mouth with one hand after she recognized the entire complex might have heard her. "I love it."

She found what she was looking for. It was a nice two bedroom with a fireplace and patio. The kitchen and dining area was pub style with an open floor plan. A high countertop divided the kitchen and dining room. Mia stood in the middle of the floor pointing, "I'll hang a huge picture here and put a flowerpot there." My heart felt fuzzy. It was her time. Mia had been my rock, and to see her eyes full of joy made me delighted. "I'll make sure to get a sofa sleeper so when you guys come for spring break you can sleep over there," she said still pointing, "and Ty can use a roll-away bed in the nursery. It's perfect."

We followed the building manager back to her office to complete the paperwork. The complex offered students of Howard a discount as a way to show their appreciation for choosing them. The double doors swung out, and the manager appeared gleeful.

"Congratulations. Both of your credit scores passed." We smiled at each other. It was official; Mia would be living in her own place in D.C. and it was all bittersweet. "When would you like to move in," asked the manager.

"Can I pay the deposit and get back to you on the move-in date? I have to ask my . . . boyfriend." From the way Mia paused and whispered boyfriend, I could only assume she wanted more.

"Welcome home," said the lady whose loud, stark voice snapped at me.

Mia and I bolted for the door. She could barely catch her breath from the sprint to the car before calling Tris. "We got it," Mia panted into the phone. From the sounds of his loud speech, I could hear through her earpiece, he was just as excited. I remembered Mia telling me how he hated the dorms and how he missed her so much. "What did he say, girl?" I asked. With a thrilled look fixed on her face and a slightly tilted head she said, "He can't wait to be with his family, again."

It was all so surreal. The only person to never judge me was leaving and would be hundreds of miles away. Vulnerability nestled in my heart, but nothing would make me see the glass half empty anymore. My new leaf was to look at life differently, see the best in situations even when they weren't obvious. I didn't cry.

Boy, oh boy, did we make the best out of that trip. We visited the capital, a few museums, and ate mounds of East Coast foods. Mia even put furniture on lay-a-way, shopped for curtains and a baby bed. Those were days to remember. My mother called me several times to see how things were going, particularly since she had to wire us money because we overspent at the malls. Finally, though, the visit ended. It was time to go home. My new life awaited me once more – the one without Mia or my Dad.

We took to the streets as soon as the sun peeked from behind the skyline to hit the long road back to Chicago. On the ride home I could think of nothing but who the heck Mother would want to live with me next.

Looking all childlike Mia said, "Turn the station, girl. That song is depressing."

"Thanks for My Child" was playing behind my dreadful thoughts of who mom would choose as my new roommate. As I scrambled through a few stations, "Mia . . ." I said, "do you ever have nightmares?"

"Don't we all, girl? . . . The station. Focus."

I giggled. "I am focused. But not just any nightmares. Nightmares about Daddy." The air got stuffy.

"Why?"

"Cuz' I would if that happened to me."

Mia paused, turned down the radio, but kept her eyes on the road. "Uh-huh . . . Yep, I do. Sometimes."

"I figured . . ." I said softly. "I'm sorry he did that to you, okay?"

"It's all good, girl. It all happened so fast . . . it wasn't your fault." Silence swallowed up the only sound left in the car. It was so quiet, the stillness became deafening.

"I miss him so much. Sometimes I feel him. I feel his strength."

"That's a good thing and I'm sure going back to

therapy is helping, too, right?"

The clouds were perfectly aligned in the sky and the weather pristine.

"Right, Tasha? . . ." Mia had to repeat her question to yank me out of my daze.

"Yep, it is," I said, as I adjusted the volume on the radio.

Biggie Smalls was on. "Turn that up, Girl," Mia exclaimed. The next thing I knew we were bumping, bouncing, and singing, "Biggie, Biggie, Biggie, can't you see . . ." along with the song.

Since we lived under the same roof, there was not much to catch up on so the music made the ride home pleasant. It was nice just being with my best friend.

§

Mia's due date came and went and she became frustrated. The thought of a C-section scared her, but being pregnant for so long made her reconsider. Mia told me how her skinned crawled every time her doctor would say, "The baby will come when it's ready." She said one day she wanted to tell him, "Did you come when you were ready because you seem like you came too early?" That was so hilarious to me.

Tris was home for summer and hung out at our place a lot of the time because he wanted to cater to Mia since he was gone most of the pregnancy. He did do a few things that led me to think he might have been seeing someone on the side, but then again, it could have been my vivid imagination. It never crossed my mind to tell Mia what I suspected. The birth of the baby was far more important.

One night it just happened. Her water broke.

"Tasha, I think it's time. Call our mothers and Tris and Ty, too, if you like," she giggled. Mia stood up from the couch and strolled slowly into the bathroom. She was extremely calm to be a teenager. I was panicking more than she was.

"WHAT DO YOU WANT ME TO DO NOW?"

Calmly as ever she said, "Call our moms and Tris."

"Oh, yeah, right . . ."

When Tris picked up I heard a woman's voice in the background so I made sure to shout loud enough just in case she could hear me, "MIA'S WATER BROKE. We're headed to the hospital." I wondered why it was suddenly silent and removed the phone from my ear to look at it. Tris had hung up.

Mia's mom waited for us in the front of the house dressed rather strangely. There was a small brown paper bag in one of her hands, a green glove on the other and she had on a suede hat that didn't match any of her clothing. Mia climbed into the backseat. Her mother flipped the mirror down on the passenger side and adjusted her petite hat. I giggled a little, but no one new why. We pulled off. A funny smell tickled my nose as I turned to see where it was coming from. Peeking through my rearview mirror I saw Mia polishing her nails, "Are you serious, sis?" I asked.

"Girl, yeah—I don't want to look ugly in there." Everyone in the car cracked up laughing.

I had no idea where Tris was coming from, but he beat us to the hospital. Since Mia was only allowed two people in the birthing room during the delivery, so I called Ty to sit with me in the lobby. I called Mom too, but like always, she didn't answer. Two hours turned to three in no time, but Ty and I played cards, watched a little TV, then he let me rest my head on his shoulder to take a nap; all the while, planting sweet subtle kisses on my forehead. That fourth hour was it. The baby was born.

Mia must be a superwoman, I thought, to have a baby

211

so quickly. I couldn't even imagine the pain she must have been in. We were all invited into her room as the nurse cleaned up the baby.

"Tasha Renee Jones," was her name. That was such an honor, "You named her after me," I asked between sniffles.

"Why not?" Tris said.

Renee was Triston's mothers' name. She passed away three years prior. Mia's mom didn't feel slighted in the least bit and appeared overjoyed that a new life was brought into the world. A tired-looking nurse came in and ended our little family reunion, "Visiting hours are over, Mia needs her rest. Dad, will you require overnight room accommodations?"

"Yes . . . Papa Dop is staying the night," Tris said as we all gathered our belongings to head home. We walked through the long hallway toward the front door as I saw my mother rushing in. "How did everything go?"

"Good. Mia is asleep, and the babys' in the nursery," I said. "Are you alone?"

"No. Dr. Beech, well, Kevin, is parking the car."

"Oh. You missed visiting hours. Maybe Kevin can pull some strings so you can, at least, visit the nursery to see Baby Tasha. She's so cute."

"Tasha, huh?"

"Yep. I was shocked, too, when they told me."

"OK, . . ." Mother strutted to the info desk to get visitor passes while Ty called his mom to inform her he'd be late. There was a knot I felt forming down in my gut. I knew no one was at my house to intervene, and Ty had every intention to take advantage of that.

And he did.

VICTIM IMPACT PANEL

Knowing Ty's mother was sitting tearfully in the back row created a boiling pressure within. My mouth sealed shut unintentionally. I struggled to fight the urge to stop the story right there and then ask permission to be escorted back to my cell. For I knew, no mother in the world would want to hear details of their child's tragedy. It was important for me to survey the room for something to focus my eyes upon. A young girl in the middle aisle, wearing a shirt with a surfer surfing, became my focal point. I stared at the large wave and drifted deeply into my own thoughts about that night—*that perfect horrible night*.

The image of us pulling up in front of my house rested in my mind's eye. Ty got out of his car and opened my door. He grabbed the lever on the left side of the seat and reclined my back as far as it would go. Kissing me all over my neck, sucking, then kissing again, he tucked his hand between my legs to pull the lever underneath it, then pushed my seat back from the steering wheel as far as it could possibly go, making sure to rub against my clit in the process. I quivered. With one leg at a time, Ty climbed on top of me, closing the door behind him so the interior light would dim. His pulsing manhood stroked about my pelvis area. His hardening and thickening could be felt through my skintight jeans. I melted with every kiss, every grind.

"Stop," I whispered in his ear but nibbling on it at the same time. I clenched his lobe between my teeth hard enough to be sensed but soft enough to tease.

"You don't want me to stop, Tasha," he said as his hand slithered underneath my shirt and bra. Licking the tip of my ear sent juices through the hole south of my navel. He licked the inside of my ear, traced the earlobe with the tip of his tongue dipping it in and out like a serpent.

"S-t-o-p," I panted even lower than before. The stops turned to moans almost to the point of sexy screams.

"Come on, babe, let's go inside." Ty opened the door once more and led me by the hand inside the house.

I tried to scamper into the kitchen. "Would you like some water?"

Ty followed me to the refrigerator unresponsive. I bent

over to grab two bottles of water from the vegetable bin at the bottom when Ty bent over, too, and kissed the tip of my back jean pocket.

"I don't want that. I want you." I was led once more by the hand to my room spellbound by my lover.

Quickly I went to the bathroom to freshen up. I came back to my room and was embarrassed when Ty turned on the TV and porn popped on. But in the end, all I stood thinking of was that moment. Still frozen in time, I recalled Ty asking if he could take off one of the condoms at least. The look I gave was enough for him to never ask that question again. I had to protect him. Since I hadn't had the heart to disclose the truth, fearing what the outcome might be, I had to be his protector. Unprotected sex was out of the question.

"Can you get on top?" he said panting irresistibly.

Watching porn taught me exactly what was expected of me. I mounted his legs, made sure both condoms were intact, and swerved back and forth vigorously. Leaning my body forward just a little to tap into the sensations from rubbing against my sensitive pearl made my knees shake. Ty groped my hips, squeezing, then releasing in no particular rhythm, helping me along with my movements. I could see him through my tightened eyes take one hand and lick his fingers before gently rubbing my nipples with his damp fingertips. My rocking and pumping got faster and faster, a tingling feeling entered my walls, and "AH ha ha" I shouted in ecstasy. I didn't even realize how fast and hard I moved, but Ty enjoyed every minute of it.

"Let it all out, baby," he said. Unaware that my body could move like that I took advantage of the feeling I gave to my love.

"Tasha, Tasha, ooooohhhhh," Ty mumbled through a closed mouth. "OH SHIT, I'm coming."

We pumped a few more times very slowly before it was over. I climbed off and lay there beside him. The thoughts of our naked, touching bodies aroused me all over again. It happened. My virginity was gone.

The facilitator of the event gave me a soft tap on the shoulders that startled me. "You only have twenty more minutes," she said softly in my left ear while holding her right hand over the ball of the microphone. "Can you continue? You look upset."

I nodded my head up and down at her, and she slid off to the side of the podium. That's when I realized I must have been standing in a daze, thinking heavily about that night.

My mind was made up; I would spare Ty's mother the details of the sex scene even though it was one of my most precious moments. I picked right up where the trouble happened; taking charge of my final twenty minutes to speak.

"You all can assume Ty and I went all the way that night. It was a beautiful thing between two young lovers. I never meant to hurt him so I asked that he wore two condoms. It was wrong. I know. But in my head I felt we would be fine with double protection. It was complete *fear* that kept me from telling him what needed to be told. Yet, at the same time, it was the most beautiful moment of my life.

When it was over, while we were spread out across the bed naked, I glanced over at his shrunken piece and noticed a small hole in the top condom. I wanted to freak out but held my composure. From what I could see, only one condom had torn. My heartbeat raced. I was petrified."

"You OK, sweetheart?" he asked me.

"Yeah . . ." I told him trying not to shiver.

Ty pulled me closer to him, and we lost the battle to our fatigue.

Sunrays beaming through the window the next morning woke me up. The cracks from the sun shining through the room gleaned directly on the condoms still worn on Ty's limp penis.

They were both ripped.

.

20 SENIOR YEAR

Senior year started off fast, and it never slowed down. Ty and I were closer than ever, but my secret was overwhelming. Mia, Tris, and the baby settled in the Washington, D.C. area and mom was so engrossed with Kevin, her fiancé, she allowed me to live in the condo alone. She told me it was very risky but was sure I could handle it, yet of course she popped up way more than I would have liked her to. That was Mom.

School hours were lonely for me though. My crew didn't exist and Ty couldn't have lunch with me anymore because studying for AP courses took up most of his time. Ty was offered academic scholarships from quite a few schools and I was proud of him, but not more proud than his mother, of course. That was her baby, her only child. Chida and I tried to pick up where we left off, but it wasn't the same. She hung out with a group of loud-mouthed girls that cramped my style. We liked each other, but sometimes circles just don't mix.

With a swag I learned to love, Ty strolled down the hall during last period, "do you need a ride, boo?" I asked lustfully.

"Naw, staying after."

"What's up with that? Day not long enough for you?"

"Gonna try out for the football team."

"Football? Boy, you ain't played football since freshman year."

Ty chuckled. "True. But I think I'm good enough to make our weak team." My eyes rolled down and lips balled up to the left with a touch of sass.

"Why the look? It's our last year . . . Why not?"

"I guess," I said unwillingly.

He kissed me on the forehead and took off down the hall to meet his boys; it was like watching a kid run to the tree on Christmas morning.

After that news, I felt a little down so I skipped last period and went home but when I entered the house, something was different. Dad's presence felt thick and dense. He was sitting on the edge of my bed, with a faint but peaceful expression, "We all make mistakes; you have to tell him."

Shaking my head vigorously from left to right, I said, "This isn't real." Never had I ever believed in ghosts or the paranormal, and besides, it was too late to tell him now, I thought. No matter what, he would hate me – I knew it. I shook off the eerie feelings and paid closer attention to the hunger pangs that spoke just as loud as my vision.

One can of chicken noodle soup sat in the cabinet looking lonely so I chose it as my snack. I was extremely bored and there was a good book I wanted to finish, so I did that, too. The end of the book was so compelling, I didn't hear my mother when she came in.

"Ma, what are you doing here?"

"I wanted to check on you, see how things were going."

"Oh . . ." So much for living alone. It didn't matter; Mom would witness me getting ready for school in the morning, that's all. *What a great way to spend her time,* I thought.

The next morning, warm water pulsating from the massage showerhead felt calming on my back as the beads of water sticking to my skin awakened me. From the distance I heard my cell phone buzzing. It was either, Mia or Ty, since no one else had the nerve to call me that early in the morning, but they would just have to wait. I wanted to dry off right there in the bathroom so the steam from the shower could keep me warm. There was no need to run out wet and get bitten by the chill of the house for an early morning call. By the time I dried, brushed my teeth, and put my contacts in, the phone was buzzing again.

Ty called twice and left a message. "I'm coming over after school," he said.

"Ma," I shouted in her direction, "Ty's coming over after school. Okay?" She didn't hear me. I finished getting dressed and figured, oh well, she'd just see him later when he got there.

When Ty arrived later that evening, I thought Mom would make a big deal about him being over so much but she didn't. The pots and pans she tossed around in the kitchen made it easier for us to have a semi-private conversation.

"Do you love me, Tasha?" It came out of nowhere so my reaction was delayed. "I mean, I know you love me, but do you love me as much as I love you?"

"Babe . . . You know I do," gushed from my mouth as I shifted in my seat a little tense.

When all else failed me, Ty was there every step of the

way, so there was nothing more I could do besides love him. But my secret sat balled flat in the middle of my stomach so penetrating it sometimes felt like it would creep up to my heart and explode. It was tearing me up inside. I lost the will to sleep and the urge to eat.

"You've been a little out of it lately."

"I know . . ." I paused a moment to eat the scoop of ice cream Ty had suspended at the tip of my mouth. A little fell on my chin; he wiped it off with the back of his hand. Ty's gestures were so sweet, so memorable. A forehead kiss followed the second scoop he fed me, then he wrapped his arm around my collar, moved closer to me, and we finished the movie that was playing. He knew there would be no breast sucking with mom cooking in the next room, although it didn't stop him from sneaking freaky touches here and there.

"Hey, Mom, what are you cooking?" I yelled. "It sure smells good."

"Turkey and chicken chili. Are you hungry?"

"YES!" we said at the same time.

From the sounds of things, she would be in there awhile. Ty took advantage of her absence, discretely reaching his hand under my shirt.

Looking back, we were being two naughty little kids and we knew better but paid it no mind.

Those types of visits became quite normal and just when I felt Ty couldn't get any sweeter; he found a new way to woo me.

Mom and I started our own tradition, one that stemmed from a regular ole trip to the mall. It was after our facials, massages, mani and pedi's Mom suggested we'd do it twice a month. I was touched. It reminded me of when Daddy would take me out for ice cream when I wasn't feeling well and it was becoming an easy task not to resent her as much.

Even though she still worked really, long hours and would leave me home alone quite often, when we did spend time together, we had fun. Time was not our enemy anymore. As soon as I realized loving my mother was so much easier than hating her, my life began to make sense. Honestly, I wasn't sure if our feelings were mutual because she often found ways to sneak low blows in every now and then. But I didn't care. Losing one parent was difficult enough and I couldn't stand the thought of losing them both. Besides, she always caught and checked her own smart remarks and would later apologize. Mom also decided it was my turn to have a real party for my birthday, and Ohhh, did she come through.

It was the party of the year. People talked about it for months. She bought tri-fold flyers for me to pass out, some of which had golden tickets inside. The people who got a golden ticket were allowed a backstage pass to meet and greet the surprise guest: Mary J. Blige. To this day, I can't tell you how she pulled that off, but she did and I wasn't surprised one bit. Doing it big was her style.

Everybody who was somebody came to the party, even Chida and her loud-mouthed crew.

Ty and I flirted all night at the party and by the look in his eyes; I may as well have been the only girl in the room because he kept his focus on me. "Babe, you are so beautiful," he said bending down close to my ear so I could hear him above the loud music.

I looked up at him with a sexy but delightful smile. It tempted him to kiss me. Mouthing, "I love you, Ty," as we rocked from side-to- side to the melody of the song, we melted. Jealous looks were plentiful across the room and everywhere I observed an eyeball was rolling here and there at us. That was when I knew I held something sweet and divine.

I thought to myself, *I'll tell him the truth after the party.* I didn't want to lose my boyfriend over a lie – a lie I had no control over. Thinking of all the ways I could tell him were playing tag in my mind.

"Ty, can I talk to you?" *No no no, that sounds corny,* I thought.

"Can you talk to me about what?" he asked.

I erupted in laughter the minute I realized my thinking out loud was becoming an issue. "Nothing. Thinking out loud *again.*"

"You've been doing that a lot lately. Better get it checked out."

"I know right. That's why I laughed."

As the song came to an end we smiled at each other and he led me by the hand to exit the dance floor. Ty was fidgeting in his pocket for something as we paced slowly to the side of the room.

"Since you think so much . . . think about this." His palm slowly opened and inside laid a shiny gold ring with the word "Promise" engraved inside. He lovingly grabbed my left hand and placed it on my ring finger. The room stood still for me. "I promise to be your friend forever, Tasha. I hope you feel the same."

"I do" rang from my mouth like he had recited his vows to me, hummmm I thought, *Mr. and Mrs. Johnson* did have a nice ring to it. We embraced each other as passion shot in and out of my soul. Something told me to look at Chida, her eyes were bucked and mouth strung open. Thinking to myself, I bet this time next week engagement rumors will be spread around school. In the end, it was safe to say, my party was a success even though Tris and Mia couldn't make it.

Ty drove his own car to the party so I didn't have to take him home. "See you tomorrow," he said.

"OK . . . love you."

He pivoted his whole body around to face me. "I love you too."

After an exchange of grins and waves we got into our cars and went home. I was elated.

Sharing personal things with my mother was never ideal since her preachy and condescending tone drove me crazy. But I needed to talk to someone, someone that knew more than anyone else. Strange as it was, I needed my mother's advice.

All I could think about on the way home were the many ways my mother could ruin the relationship we were beginning to build with her, *"I told you so, Tasha. You shouldn't have done that stupid mess, Tasha. What were you thinking, girl?"* The thoughts were so gripping, I almost changed my mind ten minutes into the ride.

Dim lights and a flickering television met me at the door. Mom and Kevin were on the couch, he was asleep, but she was focused on the screen in front of her.

"Mom, when your movie is done can I ask you something?"

She picked up the remote, muted the sound, "Sure, sweetie, what's up?"

"Not here. My room."

Without another word, she stood up, slid her feet into her pink slippers, and followed closely behind me. "I need your help," I said closing the door so Kevin couldn't hear us. Her face said, "Carry on," but she kept silent. Instantly, I regretted coming to her.

"I'm listening . . ."

I took a deep breath. "I really want to tell Ty everything. But no matter how I picture myself saying it, it just won't come out."

Mom sat on the end of my bed, folding one flap of her robe inside the other and tying the belt tightly. She tapped her hand on the mattress signaling me to take a seat. I sat. "Tasha, I don't really have a right answer for this one. All I can say is, if you love him, you have to tell him the truth."

"I know . . . but . . ."

"But what? There is no but. Either you tell him and give him a choice or you take his choices away and play God."

Everything in my being told me she was right, but it was done, we already had our special moment and now the whole thing was all too much to handle. My mom leaned over to hug me, "There isn't a right or wrong way to do it. I'm here for you no matter the outcome."

I wrapped my arms back around her. "Thanks, Cali, for giving me just what I needed, without the extras."

With a solemn face, "You're welcome, honey."

When she left my room it hit me. I was becoming a liar. The same thing I hated her so much for being. One lie after another was becoming my way of life and it weighed heavy on me – I need to take control, I affirmed.

It was settled. No matter the time or place, Ty would know the truth. Growing up wasn't all it was cracked up to be.

§

I didn't see Ty around the halls much on Monday. He practiced football directly after school every day so I went to the field, sat in the empty bleachers and watched the guys practice for half an hour or so. Ty never showed up. Immediately, I reached for my phone to check for a missed call from him but there was none.

"Mom, did Ty call or come by today?"

"No. Was he suppose to?" she asked concernedly.

"Naw . . ." I said. But I felt something was wrong.

I went to my room to change into something more comfortable.

"Tasha," my mother said through the crack in my door, "I'm not cooking tonight. We're going out. You wanna' come?"

"Yeah, sure. Be right there."

We went to Ponderosa to pig out at the buffet. I ate all types of stuff alongside my steak entrée. Oh my goodness, was I stuffed.

"We're going to do a little shopping afterwards." Mom said, "You want to go?"

"Naw. I'll pass. I need to lie down."

Kevin laughed. "You ate things that shouldn't even go

together. Nachos and egg rolls?"

That was true and funny. And from the grins planted on everyone's face, we all agreed.

I went into the house, changed clothes, and jumped right in bed and both Mom and Kevin were already gone to work when I woke up the next morning.

I staggered to the closet to pick out an outfit for school. Sliding one shirt after the other across the closet pole, because I couldn't decide what to wear, when *BOOM*, a sound so loud, it shook the building, came crashing from my living room. Glancing left and right looking for something I could use as a weapon, I stood still to hear what might come next. My cell phone wasn't within reach and I was afraid I would be heard if I tried to get to it. A small glass vase was all I saw. I picked it up and tiptoed to the doorway of my room. Not wanting to expose my entire body, I leaned my back against the door, sticking only my head out and looked left.

Before I could look to the right a pair of hands in black gloves stretched clear through the air and clutched my neck. I dropped the vase. It shattered all over the floor. My feet dangled in the air. The tips of my toes could barely touch the wood flooring. I tried to scream; "Ty, you're hurting me, please stop," but the force from his hands muffled my words. With glossy red eyes and his bottom lip stretched tightly underneath his front teeth, he said, "You knew you had that shit all along, you sick, twisted son-of-a-bitch." He kept raging, not loosening his grip at all. Through gritted teeth, he snarled, "Tell me you love me now, Tasha! Say it. I dare you."

Gurgles were all that could escape from my mouth. My chest was tightening from him blocking my air passages. "You better start praying to God," he shouted in my face, some of his spit landed on my nose.

"Ty—" I babbled. It was useless. His grip was relentless. I refused to die like that, so I started squirming about as much as I could, scratching him as his skin gathered underneath my nails. I tried to free myself from his two-handed chokehold. It wasn't working. Determined, I thought fast. With all my might, practically in midair, I jerked my knee up in one swift, hard movement to his groin, and then I came crashing to the floor. His adrenaline must have been pumping hard because the kick didn't slow him down.

As I crawled on all fours, trying to get to my cell phone, he picked up a huge, heavy floor vase from the corner smashing it into the TV. Crystal shards flew about the room. Quickly he turned; I will never forget the look on his face when he saw me attempting to escape. Ty leaped, snatched one of my legs, and dragged me on my stomach into the living room. I kicked wildly with the free foot, some of the blows landed on his chest and side. He didn't even flinch.

"How could you, Tasha?" he exclaimed.

"Ty, please . . . Don't do this." As soon as he released my leg I sprang up and took off running into my room. He gave chase.

"I'm so sorry, Ty . . . I'm so-o-o sorry," I cried uncontrollably.

He tried to hit me, and I ducked. In a fit of rage, Ty knocked over my bookshelf, punched a hole in the wall, and stomped my phone into tiny fragments. There was nothing more I could do besides cower in a fetal position trying to protect my vital organs, in case he completely lost it.

Ty stormed over to where I was, hovered over my trembling body, balled his fist, and swung once more. And again, I ducked. His hand crashed through the window. The impact of the glass must have snapped him back into a semi normal state of mind because he moved away from me, blood dripping everywhere. For some reason, I jumped up to follow him, to plead my case. The glass on my lap from the broken window fell to the floor and crunched beneath my feet. I pulled on his arm.

"Ty, please . . ."

He turned around with the look of death on his face. "Don't touch me!" he said. "Don't you ever fucking touch me! You're dead to me." He left my room and entered the living room. Ty stepped right on top of the front door like he hadn't even kicked it down. My heart felt like it would stop and I'd die in the very spot my father did.

§

I didn't call my mother. Instead, I called a repairman to come by to fix the door and window; there was nothing I could do about the TV and vase. In fact, I didn't have the energy to clean either of them up from the floor. When the repairs were completed, I called Ty sixty times or more to no avail. After calling around a few places, one of my schoolmates told me about the sports physical the team had the week before; she said maybe Ty wasn't at school because without the physical they wouldn't be allowed to play in the first game. It all made sense.

My mom found me that evening in a ball on my bed. Exhausted and tired of playing the victim, I couldn't cry anymore. She came in my room, sat on the edge of the bed, AGAIN. "I know what happened. Ms. Johnson called me a few minutes ago. She was pretty upset."

"What am I to do now, Mom," I asked in pain.

"I don't know, but first, I need Kevin to reach out to her. His trailblazing research has been keeping us alive and healthy, and we need to offer the same to Ty." Mom sighed. "I'll make sure she never gets one bill for his treatment."

Just then my bedroom door cracked open and Dr. Beech stepped in and agreed with Mom. "I sure won't charge them a dime."

I was extremely embarrassed. Too ashamed to hug them and too humiliated to thank them either, I hung my head in humiliation. Without touching the mess in the living, Mom and Dr. Beech headed directly to the Johnsons' house.

Upon their return, my mother offered very little details about the visit and of course, Dr. Beech's confidentiality oath didn't allow him to speak of it either. He didn't share one word of what he and Ty discussed. All Mother said was, "Ms. Johnson wanted badly to refuse the help, but knew it was in Ty's best interest to take it." With Ms. Johnson's income, she would never have been able to afford top-notch care for Ty. I wanted him to have the best even if he never spoke to me again and felt grateful to be in a position to help him.

§

School was becoming a distant memory. I was barely there anymore. It was evident I would have to go back if I wanted to graduate, but focusing on graduation was void when I thought about how bad I'd hurt my first true love. It was never my desire to hurt him but getting him to understand that seemed almost impossible. My mistake was horrible, some say unforgivable, and I would have to live with the regret for the rest of my life. But our lives weren't over.

Ty missed that week of school, too, according to Chida. When we finally bumped into each other in the halls two weeks later, I was mortified. The look on his face said he would choke me again if I looked his way. I turned my head completely. He kept walking like I didn't exist. I let him. The hatred in his eyes was obvious. There was no mistaking it.

Since he couldn't choke out a letter, my phone calls went unanswered, and eye contact with him was absolutely out of the question, I opted to write him instead. There was no other way. In no time at all, I had written Ty over twenty times. He never responded; not even to one letter and things went on that way for months. When Dr. Beech would see him for his office visits he would tell me, "Ty is doing wonderful." To me, that wasn't enough, I wanted to know more.

Ty started hanging out with Priscilla more often. Unsure if it was intentional or not, I still found myself saying, "I deserved it." To ease my loneliness I even hung out with Chida's group, but it simply didn't work out. They were just too much for me.

Going to D.C. for Christmas break was all I could think about because seeing Mia's face would be the biggest relief of all and we had a lot to catch up on.

21 CHRISTMAS BREAK

Mia was happy to see me. "Hey, girl," she said grinning hard as heck, "you look so good."

"Thanks girl. I tried." Baby Tasha was getting big. She was cute as she could be with her kissable chubby jaws. That's exactly what I did, *Muah, muah, muah* . . . She giggled. The baby took my mind off the troubles of the world. Innocent. Precious. From the absence of sound in the living room, I knew Tris wasn't home.

"Where's your boy?" I asked.

"He went to the store to pick up a few things. Come in the kitchen, girl. Time to catch up."

I followed Mia to the tall bar stool she bought for her pub-style counter and took a seat. It was interesting watching her every move as a new woman. To me, she was normal. The way she opened the pantry door to grab hot cocoa mix even had a normal look to it. I envied her.

"So where's Ty? You drove all this way by yourself?"

"Yep."

"Wow, how you've grown. I just knew he wouldn't be too far behind you, Mr. and Mrs. Inseparable."

"Naw, he's not coming."

"Oh, that's too bad. Tris was looking forward to having another guy around again. We bought the roll-away for him and everything."

I couldn't tell Mia Ty hadn't spoken to me since September. So I brushed it off and pushed the conversation in a different direction. "How's motherhood treating you? College, too?" I asked.

Our roles reversed. It used to be me telling all the stories as Mia asked the questions. Then it was the other way around as I played switch-a-roo on her. Mia had lots to say, too. She talked for about thirty minutes straight. Hearing uplifting news was just what I needed. We were back to our normal selves as if there had been no separation.

RING. RING

She bustled into the bedroom to pick up the phone and all I heard was, "Uh-huh, OK, sure, will do, OK, talk to you later, see you soon." Mia came rushing back to the kitchen all excited. "That was your boo."

"Really?"

"He's on the road. He said you left 'em."

My mouth dropped. "What? Is that all he said?"

"Yep. Why? What's up with y'all?" Mia said giggling. "Are you two having a relationship squabble?"

If only she knew. It was far more than a squabble; more like war of the exes. Never could I have imagined how that night would turn out so I quickly changed the subject. I wasn't too sure Mia bought it because she knew me well and I figured it wouldn't take her long to figure out I was avoiding specific questions. But the baby demanded so much of her attention that she was easily distracted.

"So, what was I saying?" Mia asked confused. Saved by short-term memory loss, I thought. Since she couldn't remember, I gave her a new subject to discuss, omitting Ty's name intentionally.

It was five or six hours later before he arrived. Dinner was over with, and we had on pajamas by the time the doorbell rang. My heart stopped.

"Hey, what up, man?" Tris said as they high-fived. "Come on in, boy. We thought you changed your mind."

Ty strolled in. I wasn't sure if anyone else saw the chip on his shoulder, but I did. "Hey, Mia," he said while giving her a big hug and lifting her off the floor a bit. "Hey, Ty, looking good there," Mia told him. Ty walked on into the house and said, "H-E-Y, Tasha . . ."

Just as I was about to acknowledge his greeting, he marched right past me heading towards the baby. That's when I realized he was speaking to her and not me.

"She's getting big, Tris. Hey, li'l girl, I was there the day you were born." Ty said to the baby as she touched the tip on his nose.

He sat down on the couch with Tasha on his lap. Tris, being the outspoken person he'd always been, "Do I smell trouble in paradise?"

Ty laughed it off. "We're okay, man, how's college life treating you?" He changed the subject just as fast as I had with Mia hours earlier. More than sure my uneasy glare told the truth about us, I turned my head the other way to keep the peace.

"College cool, dude. Same stuff, different place, you know what I mean. You should apply here."

"I don't know, man; it's an option." Ty scooted to the edge of the couch to put the baby on the floor on her little mat and picked up a magazine from the table. His performance was stellar. The way he was acting I even believed there was nothing wrong. There wasn't one thing I could think of to say to him, even though I loved him more than words could explain.

"Ty, you hungry? I can whip you up something quick since we ate already," Mia offered.

"No thanks. Appreciate the gesture but I picked up something on the road."

Jumping right in and taking my chances, "Why didn't you ride with me? We could have talked on the way," I blurted out.

Not even so much as a double blink, he replied calmly, "I'll talk to you later, Tasha," then began flipping through channels on the TV. Our eyes never connected.

If another second had gone by I would have said way more than needed, but Mia came back into the room at the perfect time with the game of Operation in her hand. Shaking it from left to right in all our faces, "Y'all know what time it is," she said cheerfully.

"Get your coins ready, Ty," Tris instructed. "I'm 'bout to spank that ass for the first time!"

"Yeah, right, dude, come on with it. Ain't none of y'all wobbly hand having people ever beat me."

Everyone in the room smirked while anxiously

searching for loose change. We gathered around the living-room table, "same rules apply," Tris said as Mia set the timer on her phone.

We all knew what that meant. It was time to determine who would go first, second, third, and fourth in the actual game. Ty always won the spot of fourth place because he had the steadiest hand, but unbelievably that time, he lost. It was the very first time Ty ever landed himself in first position, and of course I blamed myself for his game being thrown off.

"Ah, told your ass I'm gon' spank you," Tris blurted.

The game was on. The night flew by as we laughed at each other trying to get the funny bone out of the red nose board game.

"No—no—" Mia shouted while Tris banged with balled fist on the table in an effort to distract Ty. *Bang, bang, bang . . .* Tris beat his fist rapidly and hard.

"Man stop cheating," Ty yelled. "Y'all bogus."

He was about to do it again, beat us all. His game face was on, and he did it. Ty pulled the funny bone out without making the buzzer sound.

"Dang, this dude's just unstoppable with his rock-head ass," Tris joked.

"You don't wear jealousy well man; don't match your skin color," Ty responded with a joke of his own. Ty won all the money and surely didn't split it with me like he used to do.

Tasha fell asleep in her playpen while the older folk acted like children. "We're gonna' go to bed," Mia said curving her back as she yawned. "We try to make it a habit to sleep when she does."

"We understand, good night," I said nervously because I had no idea what Ty would do when they left.

"Ty, there's a roll-away bed in Tasha's room. We'll take her in the room with us while you guys are here."

Ty replied with a simple, "Cool."

Mia and Tris took off, and Ty didn't waste a single minute. "Come go for a walk with me, Tasha."

My first thought was to stay put. He had kicked my door down, choked me until I turned purple, and evil bled through his eyes the last time I saw him. I wasn't confident he could be trusted. But then again, I thought, *"who was I to talk about trust?"* My jacket and shoes were nearby. I slid them on and followed Ty out the door.

We barely passed the threshold of the complex before he went hard on me; "I drove all the way to D.C. to tell you how much I hate you." His words had a lethal sting. "You ain't shit," he continued. "Wasted flesh . . ." he hollered. I stopped walking not wanting to get too far from help if I needed it. "SAY SOMETHING!"

"What do you want me to say, Ty?" I asked fearfully.

"What the hell do you mean what do I want you to say? Say what the hell you should have been saying before fucking my life up."

There was nothing I could do or say. "Ty, I AM SORRY," is that what you want to hear?

"Wear two rubbers—wear two rubbers my ass!"

"Ty, wait . . ." I interrupted. "Give me a chance to tell you—"

"GIVE YOU A CHANCE? Give you a chance to tell me what? Don't believe what I'm hearing. I gave you four damn years to tell me. Ha—but you didn't. Now you got a shit load to say. Please, spare me and get-the-fuck-outta-here with that bullshit." He shifted his body restlessly to look me square in the eyes. A tear fell freely from his face.

"I trusted you, Tasha. How could you do me like this?"

I wanted so bad to touch him, hold him in my arms. Instead, I extended my hand toward his cheek to wipe away the tears.

SLAP!

Ty whacked my hand down to the point of burning. "Don't touch me. Don't you ever fucking touch me."

We walked in silence for a few minutes toward Mia's apartment. There was nothing I could think of to say that would make things easier for him. Nothing I could say to make it all disappear. It was one of those mistakes that crushed you, made you question your self-worth. Picking up my pace in fear of things getting uglier, I trotted ahead of Ty before taking a seat on a bench because it felt like my knees would buckle beneath me. When he caught up, Ty sat down beside me with silence being the only distance between us.

"Look . . . I only came here for two reasons. One, to tell you I don't give a damn who you tell your business to, but I don't want you telling anyone about me."

"I understand," I whimpered. "I won't, Ty. I will never betray your trust again."

"Two, I don't think my mother will ever get over this. She wants me to press charges."

"Press charges?" I exclaimed.

"You heard me. YEAH . . . charges. You know . . . JAIL."

I was stunned. "Ty—Ty—wait. You know I didn't mean to hurt you. You know this," I shouted.

"What you meant to do was destroy my life so it could be messed up like yours."

"Wait a minute. I won't let you say that. I can't believe you just said that." He was ripping the little feelings I had left right to shreds. Ty knew I loved him more than life itself. He also knew I had one hell of a life of my own and the last thing I'd want was for him to suffer. I reached across the bench to touch his face. He shoved my hand away again. "Ty, please . . ." He stormed off into the night. My body didn't have any more fight left. I put my head down, shaking it from side to side. "I'm so sorry, I'm so, so sorry," I sobbed.

From ten feet or so in front of me Ty jolted his body around and said, "I shouldn't have choked you that day. But I hate yo' ass."

It was done.

I followed behind him like a lost puppy; twisting the promise ring he gave me around and around on my finger. From somewhere I pulled some strength to think of what my dad would do. He would want me to fight back, stand up and not feel sorry for myself. "No more victim," I repeated in my mind over and over. "No more victim!"

After the blowup, I never expected Ty to stay for the rest of the vacation. But he did. Tris and Mia were two of his best friends, and what we had going on didn't change that. We made the best of it, but Ty took extra precautions to make sure he avoided any direct contact or conversation with me. I was okay with it. It was better than fighting and I understood I'd really screwed up that time.

That night, after everyone had gone to bed, I penned Ty another letter. My hope was that he didn't rip it to shreds without reading it; yet, I didn't allow my hopes to rise very high either. Looking around the apartment for one of his bags, I spotted his jacket draped across the back of the couch. I placed the letter in the front zipper pocket after puckering my lips to the page leaving a lipstick stain on the paper.

It was months before I ever heard from Ty again.

§

With my jacket still on my back, purse in hand, and mouth running a-mile-a-minute telling my mother how urgent it was to speak with Ms. Johnson, I could hardly think straight.

"She wants to press charges," I exclaimed.

"Press charges?"

"Yep. We gotta go talk to her."

"Calm down now. We can't be too hasty. She does have a right to be angry, sweetheart."

"I know," I said. "But, dang, what will jail do? It damn sure won't cure us." Mom redirected me promptly.

"Now watch your mouth, girl."

"I'm sorry." I said quickly, "but let's go."

Mother headed to the kitchen, picked up her phone, and dialed Ms. Johnson.

"Hey, how are you? It's Mrs. Beech, Tasha's mother," I heard Mom saying to her. My mother stood in the middle of the floor moving her head up and down, then left and right, silently agreeing and disagreeing with whatever Ms. Johnson was telling her.

"I understand," she said. "OK, great. Thank you so much. We'll be there shortly."

With my knee bouncing up and down, I sat anxious in my seat, eager to hear what Ms. Johnson had to say. "She's leaving soon with only a few minutes to spare." To me that was good news. Fifteen minutes was all I needed. We gathered our things and advanced toward the door.

Everything that could go wrong went wrong at the Johnson house. Her stern eyes pierced my skin and my apologies leaped around the room untouched. It actually took less than ten minutes for her to break me down even though I tried to stand firm. The conversation was deadlocked, but I refused to let her see me cry. For I knew if I could jump into a time machine and change what happened that night, *I would.* But I couldn't. Talking to Ms. Johnson finally helped me to see the blame was not all mine, though I highly doubt she intended to do that. But hey, I hadn't raped him; he was game from the very beginning. We made love that night and what I did with him wasn't an act of wickedness. What was meant to be an act-of-love turned into hate, but personally, I was tired of running from it. Hiding. Lying.

Telling Ms. Johnson how sorry I was didn't move her and I didn't expect it to. All I wanted was for her to let Ty decide on my punishment. She still had no idea how bad he choked me out. We kept that from her. However, after we spoke, I was relieved to know I could finally face my fears and move forward. Mother thanked Ms. Johnson for her time and gave her a slight head nod to acknowledge her pain, one mother to another mother. A hug seemed more appropriate for me, so I reached out to embrace her. She hugged me back, but it was without affection.

We left.

The car ride back home was silent like many past rides Mom and I had taken together. We were fine with it, though. If only Ty would hear my side of the story maybe he could learn not to hate me. Maybe, just maybe, he would go with me to group one day. We didn't have to go as boyfriend and girlfriend, just friends; the same friends we'd been since the sixth grade. But what I did broke all codes of our friendship. It was a mistake. A grave error, a fault I would regret for the rest of my life.

"Mom," I burst out, "Ms. Johnson didn't mention anything about pressing charges. Do you think she will?"

"I don't know, sweetheart. Let's just hope for the best." Mom's sorrow flipped and anger replaced it in one spilt second. "If anyone," she shouted, "and I mean *anyone*, should be locked up like an animal, it should be that bitch of a secretary, Sheila." It became obvious Mom still carried a deep-rooted anger in her heart for that woman. Looking at her in pity, I realized I didn't want that for myself and surely didn't want it for Ty. I had to find a way to get him to forgive me so we could move on.

22 PICKING UP THE PIECES

Walking the halls of the school was a task. I always
wondered what the other kids thought. Who knew what? Or
was anyone gossiping about me. One day Chida crept up to
me from behind. "Girl, why don't I see you with Tyrone
anymore?"

"A-n-d hello to you too, Chida," my mouth shot out
sarcastically.

"I'm sorry, girl. That was dead rude of me, huh? All in
yo' Kool-Aid and don't know the flavor. You good?"

"Cool . . . I'm good," I said. "But to answer your
question, Ty's not feeling me right now."

"Go figure. When you come east, he scurries west."
Her observation was unwanted and annoying, but by then,
keeping my cool came easy.

"C'mon, now. The cutest couple in school. Our Usher
and Chilli." Somehow I managed to pull off a half grin.
"Hey, Chida, look, I'm running late, but can you do me a

favor?"

"Maybe . . . Naw, I'm kidding. What . . .?"

"When you see Ty can you tell him I said I'm sorry?"

"For what?"

"Never mind all that, will you do it?"

"Sure, chica, whatever you need." A little hope set in, and we parted ways. Ty would know just how serious I was when Chida told him what I said because he knew I would never tell her any of my business with her blabbermouth crew in tow. It was left at that. Besides, another guy from school had been pushing up on me at the time. His name was Greg.

Greg had a little more urban swag than Ty. He was no dummy either, but I didn't mind his street slang entering our conversations from time to time. He was shorter than Ty, lighter than Ty, and how can I put this? Umm, He just wasn't Ty. They were polar opposites. But in his own right, he was cute and owned his personality, which I liked. In the beginning I would blow him off, hoping someday Ty would forgive me, but that day seemed centuries away and it came easier to put that thought out of my mind.

Eventually, the hi's and bye's between Greg and I grew into chats and walks, and in time, we were pretty close friends. Ty had my heart, but since I couldn't have the one I loved, I loved the one I was with.

Valentine Day was approaching. It was interesting to see how Greg treated his ladies. Placing price tags on gifts was never my thing because that's how Mom did me, so he would lose some major points if he bragged about prices. But if his thoughtfulness shined through it would surely add a plus to his scorecard.

Who knows what possessed me to call Ty and invite him to the dance even though I knew Greg was really feeling me, but it was a huge mistake. To my surprise, he picked up his phone for me, something he hadn't done in months, and Greg swiftly faded in the background.

"You finally picked up . . ."

"What's up, Tasha?" Ty replied in the dullest of voices.

"How have you been? I missed you."

"Wow," he said sarcastically, "what a question. How the heck else you think I've been?" After hearing his response, I didn't know where to go next so I went for the gusto.

"We used to be friends. I know I hurt you, but—"

"But what?" he said, rapidly chopping me off. In a

more timid voice than before I continued, ". . . but you treat me so cold now."

"A-n-d? . . . You said that to say what?" Deep inside I wanted to ask him to the dance, but my pride wouldn't allow it. Since he was actually giving me some talk time, I thought of a more positive question to ask him instead. In hindsight, to me I thought it was a constructive idea, he didn't.

"Would you like to go to group with me sometimes?"

"H-u-h?"

"Group. You know, where people sit and talk about things."

He grunted as if I was trying to take him to a cheerleading competition or something. It was obvious his patience had worn thin. "Look, Tasha, didn't I tell you," he shouted, "that I don't care who you tell your business to, but you better not tell mine?"

"Yeah, but—"

"But what? There is no but. You tell anyone and my mother is sure to move forward with her plans."

"Ty, wait a minute. This is different. These are people who suffer—"

Ripping off my sentence like a page from a book, Ty

exclaimed, "I could care less what they suffer from. I don't want to talk to anyone about shit."

In an effort to calm him down, I gave up totally on bringing up the dance. "Ty, I just want better for you than me. That's all."

"I might have believed that had you told me the truth from the beginning. Now you can't tell me shit. As a matter of fact, I'll see you around."

Click. He hung up. Some might say his answering the phone was progress, but I knew Ty better than that – It wasn't.

Going to the dance with Greg wasn't half bad, especially when Ty came strolling in with Priscilla on his arm. Outrage wasn't the word for what I felt when I saw them together as I stared at them feverishly.

"Yo, you're a cutie, Tasha," Greg said jerking my attention from Priscilla to him.

"Thanks."

"What time you wanna' blow this joint? It's kinda' lame," He was right, it *was* on the lame side.

"C'mon, let's go." Greg led me out of the room by my hand. The steam from Priscilla's eyeballs boiled the hairs on my neck as we left.

Opening up to Greg came easy. He had an older soul. In a way, his directness reminded me a little of my father even though I realized I wanted any and everything to remind me of my dad with the way things were going in my life. Except my father wouldn't have been caught at all using words like, "Yo, trill or sucka." That part of Greg was the uniqueness that I came to adore.

One night our conversation got so intense I asked him how much he knew about HIV and AIDS. To my surprise Greg was quite knowledgeable. In fact, he knew so much I couldn't help but to ask, *"Are you positive?"*

"Naw, I'm not, but my uncle was. He died from it. He was my favorite."

My heart sank. "Sorry to hear that."

"It's cool, sexy. I just want to do more to help other people."

"Yeah, yeah, same here."

"But why'd you ask," he said.

Stuck, not wanting to say too much and blow my own cover, I instinctively retorted, "I saw you at the walk, remember?"

"Yep. Sure do." It was weird. On the one hand, I was getting stronger, but something still tingled at the thought of disclosure. Maybe it was because I could never forget that Ty did threaten me to sworn secrecy with physical and deadly force.

Although Greg could never replace Mia, or Ty, even, he was my safety blanket. He understood me. And as the school year drew to a close, the ordinary stresses of prom and graduation took its course. I knew Greg would be my date, but what I dreaded most were the traditional after-prom rituals. It is widely known that many kids had sex after prom, but I was terrified. What happened between Ty and I could never happen again, I reassured myself as my social stressors multiplied by ten.

It was spring break, though; time to see Mia, Tris, the baby and the perfect opportunity to put my worries aside and have some fun. Oh how I missed them and couldn't wait to take on the highway again.

§

Guilt would swoop in and swoop out of my chest just thinking about all that had gone on that I kept from Mia. She knew nothing. To fill the gaps of our talks where I would usually speak about my life was replaced with stories of how Tasha scoots around on the floor. Or how the baby begged for food anytime anyone entered the kitchen.

"Eat, eat . . ." Mia said she would say. It just didn't feel right to mention my heartbreaks which would reduce her excitement of motherhood, so I never said anything.

Visiting my extended family was long overdue even if I never made one reference to my crazy life. Never in a million years did I think Ty would show up after he bawled me out at Christmas vacation. Yet, he called.

"What a surprise. I'm glad you dialed my number," I said as soon as I pressed the talk button.

"Hey. Last time you said we could ride together. Does the offer still stand?"

The most shocking look appeared on my face. "Yeah, sure. Why not?" I said, struggling to sound normal. The initial shock was nothing compared to the nervousness overtaking my spirit.

"You're sure? You ain't said five words to me in four months. That's less than a word a month."

"Can I ride with you or not?"

If Ty could have seen the frowns on my face he would've changed his riding arrangements immediately, but I managed to murmur, "Sure."

"Cool. See you Friday. I'll park at your place."

"Okay . . ."

Click. He hung up on me again. I didn't know whether I should be happy, sad, scared or defensive. When I spoke to Greg later that evening, "Guess what? You're not going to believe who called me and what they said."

"Don't tell me," Greg said amused, "Tyrone?" The boy started laughing so violently I thought I was crazy.

"What's so funny?"

"Sorry, baby, I'm not laughing at you," he simmered down a bit. "I'm laughing at the situation."

Oddly enough, I didn't realize there was a situation. I was confused.

"My ex called me yesterday, too, talking all willy-nilly."

"Really?" I asked kind of jealous.

"Yep. She wants to holla' at me in person."

All types of questions shuffled in my head, but I kept them to myself. Looking at the glass half-full, it was a good thing Greg's ex wanted to talk privately. It would save me the embarrassment of telling him my secret if they decided to get back together. And, if Ty suggested on our ride back to D.C. that we should get back together, I would be free to do that, too.

"Okay, hummmmm, so we'll have lots to talk about when I get back from my trip then, right?" In between a chuckle and a cough Greg agreed and we left well enough alone.

Ty was always a prompt young man. If he said five o'clock, he would arrive at 4:50. My mother was aware he was coming and on her best behavior when he arrived. He appeared to enjoy her small talk by the pleased look on his face, but I knew not to get to comfortable. My mother could be explosive, and she hadn't forgotten how Ms. Johnson treated me that day we went to speak to her. So it was in my best interest to keep an open ear on their conversation, just to make sure it didn't take a turn for the worse. That was the last thing I needed.

"I'm ready," I said to Ty.

"Drive safe, you guys," Mom stated. "Try to have some fun."

"Thank you, Mrs. Davis, I meant Mrs. Beech," Ty said placing a magazine back on the table.

"See you later, Ty. I love you both."

We walked toward the car like the odd couple. Neither

one of us said a word. After climbing in the truck, Ty connected the GPS and buckled his seat belt as I adjusted the mirrors and found mood music. We needed something to listen to that would disrupt the thick tension inside the car.

"This is weird."

Ty tilted his head, "What's weird?"

"You asking to ride with me. What brought that on?" I asked, trying to be passive but failing at it.

Ty's response was in sync with his judgmental glow. "So I'm not good for a ride . . . Go figure," he said pulling a cough drop from his pocket and tossing it in his mouth.

"A ride, huh . . . You're something else, you know that." Not sure if I had the right to get angry I attempted to hold back. "Sure, you can ask for a ride, Tyrone. It was just out of the blue, that's all."

"You're overanalyzing it. It's just a ride."

Without hesitation, I snapped back quickly, "But this is my car!" My reaction was venomous and caught him off guard. I saw red in his eyes.

"Look, Ty, I made the worst mistake of my life when I kept that from you. But will you hate me for the rest of your life? Or, better yet, sit here and pretend that you weren't a willing participant in the matter. If so, that's on you." I knew my reaction was risky but since being nice to him had no effect, I tried a new tactic.

Surprisingly, he didn't offer up a rebuttal. He sat quietly like a student listening to review questions right before an exam. I took advantage of his attention. "I had to forgive some people, too, you know. I was a virgin when we slept together. So it's not like I was some slut, whore who was reckless with my own life. How was I to know that two condoms would cause more friction? " In my mind, since Ty sat rather calm and silently, I felt I was coming across to him. So patiently I waited for him to finally let out some of his emotions. Nothing. Absolutely nothing. Not a word. "Say something, Ty."

"Turn that up," he said pointing to the radio.

Timing was not right. Ty did not care to share anything with me. Our friendship was ruined, his cold shoulder was frigid, and I needed to simply accept it and try to move-on.

We drove for three hours on nothing more than recycled songs and the sound of the wind slicing the atmosphere. Ty loved me, I knew it, but hated what I'd done to him – and you know what? I didn't blame him. It was exactly what Dad warned me of. *"Don't put anyone in your position, Tasha. "* Go figure. He was right. Ty was dealing with the same feelings I bottled in all my life. What would people say if they knew? How would they react? In fact, Ty was worse off than I was. At least I contracted it in what some might have considered a freak accident. But for Ty, his way of contraction was stigmatized. To add to the intensity, he still loved the girl who infected him, although he tried hard not to show it. Why else would he be in my car? My heart bled for Ty as we continued along the empty road. My only wish was that he would use me as his outlet like I'd done with Mia. I figured, that way we could ban together to help others instead of keeping it all inside and hurting internally.

"I gotta' pee. Let's stop."

A glow emerged on my face. "The dead has not only arisen, but HE SPEAKS," I said jokingly. Ty put on a strained grin as I hooked a right onto the next exit. "Your turn to drive when we're done."

"Yeah, whatever," he said as he trotted off into the distance.

Using the restroom was a great idea. My belly was full and tight. As I stood in the stall unbuckling my belt flashbacks returned. My mind still wandered as I peered into the mirror, washing my hands. "You can do it, Tasha. Be brave. You can't change what happened, but you can help what happens next," I said over and over again to myself. It was settled. I would try talking to Ty once more.

When he rolled onto the highway, I started with simple questions. Nothing with an open end, hoping he would open up. Surprisingly, he said a few more words than before but nothing to consider engaging. I gave up, propped a pillow underneath my chin, and went to sleep. The next time my eyes opened, we were in front of Mia's.

They were so happy to see us. It was obvious the baby didn't remember who we were. She reached for her mom to pick her up and refused to get down. Every time I neared her, she would place her little head gently on Mia's shoulders and look the other way. I thought it was cute.

It was an ordinary trip. We played our regular games, talked, and enjoyed each other's company. Ty wasn't as rude to me as he was the last visit. But I did feel his cold shoulder, although I never let any of them see me sweat. And when I finally accepted the fact that Ty would never ask me as his date to the prom, it became evident I would tell him Greg and I was going together.

"I don't care who you go to the prom with," he snarled

at me in the car on the way home.

"Damn, Ty, I'm trying here," I shouted. "Please don't let our friendship go, at least."

"Whatever, man." Those were his last words before the deadly silence returned.

Buzz around school, Ty was taking a cheerleader to prom anyway. He didn't tell me though. Instead, we just endured another long ride in the mighty world of awkwardness. When I drove, he slept. He drove, I slept. So much for conversation I thought.

When we made it to my house my mom and her new husband were leaving. "Where are you guys going," I said to them as I gathered my belongings from the backseat.

"To check on the house and pick up a few things. How was the trip?"

"Cool."

"It was all right," Ty uttered.

"Good. We'll be back shortly."

I waved good-bye to my parents as Ty transferred his things from my car to his.

"You want to come upstairs for a while?" One more desperate attempt I tossed out.

"Naw. I'm good. See you at school." It was

extremely obvious Ty would never forgive me. He walked away without saying good-bye.

In a voice lower than a whisper I said, "Bye, Ty." I knew it was all over and done with.

My friendship with him was ruined.

.

23 THE PRICE I PAID

"Hahahaha," the conversation was so juicy. Greg and I were on the phone cracking up at the story of our lives. Our exes really dropped bombs on us. Prom, graduation, and going to *another level* all surfaced in a single conversation.

My pulse dropped. *Shit!* I thought. Not again. Not so soon. Once more, my insides were jilted but without any further hesitation, I said it. *Boom*, it was done. Greg didn't even drawback.

"So that's why there were red ribbons in the gift bags at Mia's party, huh?" he began pitching questions in the air. "I thought that was pretty odd for a party bag." He kept speaking aloud, to himself. "That's why you were at the walk? . . . OH, that's why you asked me did I have it?" It was like watching Greg piece a puzzle together. I never made another sound. Then there was an uncomfortable silence. My stomach roared thinking he would ask me did I give it to Ty.

". . . Is that why Ty broke up with you?" Time stood still. All I could see were two huge hands clenching my throat again if I told Greg the truth. Next time he just might kill me, I figured.

"H-e-l-l-o? You there?"

"I'm here . . ."

"Oh, you got quiet on me."

"Ump . . ." was all I could say.

"So, Ty just called it quits without even trying huh? Wow. So much for believing in Magic Johnson's wife." I could hear Greg fumbling with a piece of paper, but he kept right on discharging his thoughts aloud. "So dude left you cuz' he didn't want to catch it? What a punk. But, um, I guess I do understand him though. There are risks involved."

My eyes popped open. I never thought of putting it that way. But since Greg said it, that's what I ran with.

"Yeah . . . kinda," I said, not wanting to tell another lie I'd be forced to cover up later.

"Don't take this the wrong way, but I guess you can't blame him for being scared."

"Naw . . . I don't."

"But doesn't he know there's ways he could protect himself?" Greg continued his solo conversation as my mind wandered ferociously. Telling Greg went so well, I could only imagine how things might have gone had I given Ty the same chance.

"Yeah . . . but you know what? We both know lots of people who wouldn't understand." I said. "It is what it is."

"True. So . . . umm . . . I guess this means we should hold off on that next level thing for now," he chuckled.

Shrugging my shoulders intensely although Greg couldn't see me, I responded, "Guess so."

Greg's experience with my situation made things so much easier for us to bond. He didn't judge me. I felt comfortable sharing some things with him. Life as I once knew was finally over. I knew my father was looking down on me smiling, "There you go, baby girl." The problem was my soul hadn't given up on Ty. I still loved him. My heart belonged to him, even though Ty wanted nothing more than to rip it out of my chest. Literally.

§

Going back to school after laying it all out to Greg was easy. I had some sore days, knee pains, and eye pains, but pressed forward. The finish line was in sight. No matter what

happened later on down the road we call life, I knew mine
finally had meaning. I found my voice. Eventually, Ty began
speaking to me when we'd pass each other in the hall. I did
nothing more besides return the greeting. I learned to accept
what became of us. Prom came and went. Just as I had been
told, Ty took one of the cheerleaders, but it didn't hurt as
much seeing them together because Greg had a way of
demanding my undivided attention. We had fun anytime we
hung out.

My mom started making a big fuss about a huge
graduation party. I strongly rejected the idea. Getting my
diploma was more than enough reward for me after four long,
hard years. It was the simple things I came to enjoy. Instead,
opting for a nice dinner at my favorite steak house was the
better choice so that's what we did. Mia, Tris, my mom,
stepdad, and Greg all went out to eat. We chatted happily.
Everyone looked upon me with such proud faces and I even
felt quite proud of myself.

In the corner of my eye, I saw a waiter wheeling a chair
toward our table and it rattled my nerves a bit thinking it was
Ty coming to ruin everything. Oh how I hoped my
assumption was wrong. Just as I figured the worst was about
to happen, the beautiful gold chain and diamond earring I had

delivered to Ty as a graduation gift rushed in my mind. The note inside the perfectly wrapped box begged once more for his forgiveness, but all I got was a simple text in return, "THANK YOU." So I wondered had he come to the restaurant to thank my mom and me in person. He knew I couldn't afford it without her. But how did he know where we were? I was totally confused and worried.

Greg's phone rang a number of times as we sat patiently waiting for the waiter to arrive at our table. Mia was adjusting a large bib on Tasha's neck and my mother's face blazed with joy once the secret was revealed. It was a human-sized wax replica of my father. My mother had it custom made so he could be seated at the table with us. At first sight, I was creeped out. It never will cease to amaze me the things my mother did. She slid her chair from underneath the table, stood up in her tight pencil skirt that hugged her hips, and pointed her glass towards the ceiling. We picked up our glasses to join her.

"I know this has been a long, rough road for all of us, but we lost a great man along the way. John Davis was one of the best fathers to ever live. Speaking for us all, I know he would have given anything to be here with Tasha tonight. I saw your faces. It might seem strange, but this was my way to say he is, and will always be, here to celebrate his daughter's accomplishments. Cheers to the man of the hour—John."

Clink, Clink, Clink.

The toast made me feel warm and cozy inside. To me, my dad was there in spirit, with or without the wax figure. It was then I saw love in Mom's eyes. Not just for me but for my father, too. She had finally moved beyond her own hurt and I knew a brand new beginning was not too far ahead. The night was grand. Everything was so deep and moving that I never saw Greg leave the table as Mia and I took turns feeding the baby mashed potatoes. Tasha kicked her little feet in the high chair after every scoop. Scanning the restaurant curiously, I spotted Greg in the corner by the restroom on his phone looking troubled and as I walked toward him he turned his head slightly in the opposite direction. A sullen expression took over his demeanor.

"Is everything Okay?" I asked.

Greg's eyes were pulled toward a piece of loose thread hanging from his shirt. "No."

"What happened? Who is that?"

He was jammed. Couldn't move. It disturbed me a little.

"Tasha . . ."

"Tasha, what? You're making me nervous." Greg wore

that sorrowful look in his eyes I knew far too well. "What, Greg . . .? Just tell me," I shouted. "Trust me, I can handle it." My mouth kept running. I was losing my cool, drawing attention our way.

"Ty's mother pressed charges against you."

"She *w-h-a-t* . . ." I uttered in total shock.

I was so embarrassed. The truth was out. There was no way I wanted Greg to find out the truth that way and I cared about how he felt, but it didn't stop my anger. "W-H-A-T?" I said through gritted teeth and a slight pop of the neck. This time my mother heard me and headed our way.

"How do you know? Who t-t-t-old you that?"

"My sister . . ."

I couldn't believe what I was hearing. I was being exposed to the world. Why would she do such a thing? Prison won't help me, I thought as I stormed out of the restaurant enraged.

"Tasha! Wait! Where are you going?" I heard my mother yell across the parking lot.

"To talk to Ms. Johnson."

"Wait! Stop just one minute," Mother pleaded.

I halted right in my tracks to hear her out. "This woman is obviously crazy," I screamed waving my hands madly with each word.

"We are *not* going to talk to her," Mom declared. My eyes whizzed in her direction in a flash.

"What do you mean . . .?"

"We tried that already, remember, sweetheart? It won't help." Listening to my mom's nonsense and thinking about Ms. Johnson's nonsense got more difficult as the minutes passed.

"I'M GOING AND THAT'S FINAL," I lashed back as I spun to walk away. I could hear the clacking from Mom's heels as she caught up to where I stood. She grabbed me tightly from behind, holding me close in the type of embrace you see only in movies. I turned around to hug her back.

"Well, what do you suggest?" I mumbled with my head buried in Mom's shoulder blade.

Rubbing my hair gently, as I found comfort in her embrace, she said calmly, "I suggest we go back inside and finish dinner and enjoy the rest of the evening." Her calm behavior and reasoning sounded just like my father.

All of my secrets were out. I could see Greg through the window. It was obvious he was telling Mia and Tris something. You would have thought Tris saw a ghost from the look on his face. After all these years he finally knew the truth. Mia hung her head low. Greg had no idea I never told a soul besides him and Mia before he spilled it at the table. Funny, though, I was fine with it. My body felt lighter. The weight was gone. No more secrets weighing me down. I finally understood how mom must have felt when she told me her biggest secret that day at the counselor's office. It was an odd sense of relief.

"You're right, Mom. I guess it's time I pay the price."

"Are you Okay, sweetheart?"

"Okay as I'll ever be . . ." She strung her left arm around my neck and took my right hand into hers. We went inside. I saw Mia signaling everyone at that table that we were coming and they all sat upright adjusting their posture, trying to look normal. Little did they know I was struggling to act normal, too, as I took my seat at the table.

"Honey, do you think you can take off work for a few days? I want to take the kids to Hawaii tomorrow."

"Tomorrow?" my stepfather gawked. "That's such a short notice to give the hospital."

The expression on Mom's face said the deal was nonnegotiable. My mother took my father's position in that moment. Taking me on a trip was her way not to say, "I told you so." And her way to say, "I know what John would have done if he were here." Her gesture was greatly appreciated.

Dr. Beech agreed, and we all bubbled with excitement. Mia and I looked at each other and said in unison, "H-A-W-A-I-I!" No one got the joke but us.

Hawaii was awesome. Mom got two rooms, one for the girls and one for guys. She said it would be like a sleepover that lasted a week.

I'd never seen water so blue. Mom finally got it. Being one with the water gave me an unexplainable feeling and that trip to Hawaii made up for her not buying me the pool when I was little. Holding little Tasha over small, rippling waves, just enough so her toes could touch the surf, was harmonious. It was relaxing watching Tris and Greg play Frisbee in the distance. Although I couldn't help but wish Ty was there instead of Greg, I accepted that chapter of my life as closed. Onward and upward, I thought. It was on that island I realized my purpose. It was meant for me to speak out. Tell my story. Since I'd been through hell and back, nothing would stop me and maybe, just maybe, Ty would forgive me one day, too. I sat in the sand, Tasha on my lap, and we enjoyed the splashes from the warm waves.

VICTIM IMPACT PANEL

Staring out into the audience, confident and true, I said, "I can take your questions now." Hands went up all across the room. Cameras flashed. People talked. Some were even crying and scrambling in their purses for tissues.

I'd done my duty. When the Q&A ended, the room thickened with standing bodies. I saw Ms. Johnson's purple shirt squeezing through the crowd, maneuvering her way to where I stood at the podium. Halting the fear that tried to erupt, I thrust my shoulders back and held my head up high.

By the time I had her full body in scope, I realized she could barely hold it together. My story had moved her, too. She reached out for me with both arms, wrapping them tightly around my back. "I hope you can forgive me, too," she whispered.

ABOUT THE AUTHOR

Author Tisha Starr is a single mother from Chicago, Illinois. She graduated from the University of Illinois at Chicago with a Bachelor of Arts in English Literature. It was there she decided to delve into the publishing community with her cunning sense of storytelling. Tisha Starr is known for her chatty and fun loving nature and felt there was no better way to reach people than by writing things down. While working a full-time job and raising three children she completed her first novel. Those that know her best would describe her as a fearless, go-getter who never stops. She hopes many of you will become long lasting and loyal readers of her works.